HOT CHEFS

Ken Hom

Rosamund Grant

Anthony Tobin

Gary Rhodes

Bruno Loubet

Rose Gray & Ruth Rogers

Clive Howe

Darina Allen

Paul Gayler

Shaun Hill

Anton Edelmann

Antonio Carluccio

Antony Worrall Thompson

Paul & Jeanne Rankin

HOT CHEFS

*Over 150 recipes from
Britain's greatest chefs*

BBC BOOKS

This book is published to accompany
the television series entitled *Hot Chefs*
which was first broadcast in October 1991

Published by BBC Books,
a division of BBC Enterprises Limited,
Woodlands, 80 Wood Lane
London W12 0TT

First published 1992
Recipes © Contributors 1992
Compilation © BBC Enterprises Ltd 1992
Introduction © BBC Enterprises Ltd 1992
ISBN 0 563 36387 8
Designed by Tim Higgins
Recipes collated and tested by Jane Suthering
Photographs by Martin Brigdale

Set in Monotype Garamond by Selwood Systems, Midsomer Norton
Printed and bound in Great Britain by Butler & Tanner Ltd, Frome
Colour separation by Technik Ltd, Berkhamsted
Jacket printed by Lawrence Allen Ltd, Weston-super-Mare

POINTS TO REMEMBER
● Ingredients in the recipes are given in metric and imperial measures. Use either system, but never both, in one recipe.
● 1 tablespoon = 15 ml.
● Use granulated sugar unless otherwise specified.
● Herbs, fruit juices, etc are fresh unless otherwise specified.
● Always read through the entire recipe (main dish and sauce and/or dressing or other accompaniment/s) before starting to cook. The ingredients for a sauce or dressing may include, for example, meat or poultry juices from the main dish. Other recipes require an ingredient such as stock to be prepared beforehand. These 'subsidiary' recipes come immediately after the relevant recipe, with their names in SMALL CAPITAL LETTERS.

Contents

Introduction
PAGE 14

Darina Allen
PAGE 18

Antonio Carluccio
PAGE 36

Anton Edelmann
PAGE 52

CONTENTS

Paul Gayler
PAGE 72

Rosamund Grant
PAGE 88

Shaun Hill

Ken Hom

Contents

Clive Howe
PAGE 134

Bruno Loubet

Paul and Jeanne Rankin

CONTENTS

Gary Rhodes
PAGE 186

Ruth Rogers and Rose Gray
PAGE 200

HOT CHEFS

Anthony Tobin

CONTENTS

Antony Worrall Thompson
PAGE 232

Introduction

Britain is enjoying a resurgence of interest in food, fuelled by newspapers, magazines, books, luscious photography and radio and television programmes. *Hot Chefs*, which was conceived as entertainment rather than education, has taken television cookery that little bit further. Watching professional chefs at work, absorbing their ideas, their techniques and their tips, has been inspirational to more than a few viewers, judging from the letters flooding into the *Hot Chefs* office, the calls from catering colleges, and the complaints from restaurants whose entire brigades stopped work each morning to watch.

Chefs are seen as stars rather than skivvies, and the profession has become imbued with tremendous glamour. Despite the hard work involved – for cooking in a professional kitchen is stressful, uncomfortable and tiring – many young people are looking to the world of food for their future. It was not always so in Britain.

The Bad Old Days

Eating well and good food have never been as inherent in the fabric of British culture as they are in the countries of southern Europe. Geography possibly plays a part in this: in colder climates food may be regarded more as fuel than the sensual experience it can and should be. But that is not the whole answer. Although the ingredients in England and France are nominally the same, the ploughman's of the average English pub with its indifferent bread, shrink-wrapped Cheddar and limp lettuce, is far removed from what a Frenchman might be offered – a fresh baguette, a piece of perfect Brie, a tomato with flavour. French HGV drivers, those arbiters of all things gastronomic, must despair of the 'fuel' they are still offered in Britain: motorway mass catering and soggy chips with everything.

It is all a matter of expectations, and the British once seemed to have settled for a generalised second best. Eating well was seen as an extravagance. Fewer people in Britain regularly ate out in restaurants than elsewhere; when they did so, they were expected to enjoy themselves without their children. Cooking well at home seemed to be an extravagance too, particularly of time. Despite the inspirational work of many food writers over the years, there has been a mushroom growth of commercial ready prepared or chill-fresh dishes that require no more creative input than the switching on of an oven or microwave. Small wonder, then, that the British have been for too long regarded as the gastronomically dispossessed of Europe.

There was also a sense of disinheritance, for a British style of cooking did once exist. Although less regarded than that of France or Italy, it could be seen as a distinct cuisine, one which was built on the same solid foundations: good ingredients, simply and carefully cooked. But its proponents, the chefs, were regarded as little more than manual labourers, doing what was essentially women's work, and therefore, chauvinistically, to be disregarded. In Britain a mere chef would never be be considered worthy of high honour, unlike in France where Auguste Escoffier, although working in London, was presented with the *Légion d'honneur* in 1920. (Paul Bocuse was later accorded the same honour in 1975.)

The New Enthusiasm

This British gastronomic depression seems to be lifting, slowly but surely, and food had gradually been elevated from fuel to fun.

It all began in the early 1950s, with the publication of Elizabeth David's *A Book of Mediterranean Food*. Beautifully written and inspirational, it opened the eyes of a whole generation of British professional and domestic cooks to new possibilities. Raymond Postgate's first *Good Food Guide* appeared a year later, and continues to encourage excellence in restaurants and awareness of good food in their customers.

The journalism of Robert Carrier in the 1960s reacquainted the British with herbs and spices – once a strand of their native cuisine through trade and empire-building – and their use in numerous international dishes. The growth of restaurants specialising in the cuisines of the Middle East, China and India came with what one editor of the *Good Food Guide* called the 'rice bowl revolution'. If some restaurants had to adapt to the British desire for chips with everything (even chicken fried rice) and cheap food to soak up the beer, the writers who came afterwards and who introduced the true glories of these cuisines – among them Claudia Roden, Kenneth Lo and Madhur Jaffrey – soon redressed the balance. There are now many ethnic restaurants which can rank with the very best French and Italian ones.

A major element of the British food renaissance is the contribution of professionals from abroad who chose to work in Britain – among them the Roux brothers, Anton Mosimann, Raymond Blanc and Nico Ladenis. In their kitchens, many of today's hot chefs received the basic training that provided the foundation for the increasingly assured development of their own skills. And Mosimann's exploration of the culinary history of his adopted country was virtually responsible for reviving a British culinary identity. Many of the rising young stars in Britain have embraced this, moving away from the long standing shadow of French *haute cuisine*, and exploring their own native heritage.

It was not only cooks who played an important part in encouraging good cooking in Britain. Country house hotels have burgeoned since the 1970s, and their owners, passionate about food, introduced the culinary talent to match the splendours of their houses and keep their dining-rooms thriving. In doing so they opened up new arenas in which young chefs can display their skills.

The demand for excellence in the raw materials of this culinary revolution has galvanised growers, breeders and importers, and chefs have been responsible for encouraging and developing small and interesting food industries. (The products of some of these suppliers have actually inspired the chefs.) Sadly, much of this produce is expensive and remains out of reach of potential customers, at home or in restaurants. The right balance will be achieved only when these high-quality ingredients are the norm, when the British have become as righteously fussy in their food-buying as the French or Italians.

The Future

The basic foundations of good cooking and its appreciation are laid early. Almost without exception, the chefs in this book were seduced by parental, usually maternal, influence, and by a childhood introduction to well-cooked, good food. With that instilled passion for their subject, they have had the confidence to enter the profession, to explore, experiment, absorb and grow. That they, in turn, are passing on their expertise and enthusiasm is demonstrated by the keen cheerfulness of many of their young programme assistants, some of whom may well be the hot chefs of the future.

Now that the British are becoming more comfortable with, and accustomed to, the pleasures of eating, the next generation – who are children now – can also learn to appreciate good food. They may or may not choose to enter the profession. What is important is that they become enthusiastic and knowledgeable consumers, at home and in restaurants. Without that hope for the future, the culinary re-education of the British, so entertainingly counterpointed by the *Hot Chefs* programmes, could well founder.

Useful Notes

High-quality ingredients are the essential basis of the recipes in this book and it is worth taking the time to find the best that are available. Today, there is an almost bewildering choice of fresh vegetables and fruits, from the many different salad greens that appear on supermarket shelves throughout the year, to what were once considered 'exotic' tropical imports – coriander leaves, red and yellow peppers, daikon radishes, plantains, yams and sweet potatoes. Supermarkets also offer an increasingly wide range of poultry, including free-range and cornfed chickens and poussins, and fish, and a good selection of cuts of meat. You will, nevertheless, find that some of the ingredients in this book – pig's caul is an example – call for the co-operation of a friendly specialist butcher.

An Italian delicatessen will provide ingredients such as polenta, speck (a kind of smoked ham), pancetta (cured pork) and the rice used in risotto. Oriental ingredients like chilli bean sauce, rice vinegars and fish sauce are available from oriental grocers and supermarkets, while Scotch bonnet peppers and vegetables like christophene and breadfruit are sold in West Indian and African shops and markets. Many Caribbean and oriental ingredients are also available, by mail order, from Exotic Speciality Food Limited, 8 Sycamore Centre, Fell Road, Sheffield s9 2AL.

Darina Allen

Avisit to County Cork is said to be incomplete without a stay, or a meal, at *Ballymaloe House*. Its famous kitchen is overseen by Myrtle Allen, and Darina Allen cheerfully acknowledges Myrtle's influence on her own style, which she describes as Irish country-house cooking. It relies on top-class ingredients: vegetables from their own kitchen garden (Ballymaloe is virtually self-sufficient); local free-range poultry and eggs; and fresh fish caught nearby at Ballycotton. They are thrice blessed, she says. These ingredients are combined in simple and delicious ways – in wholesome vegetable soups, in poached mackerel with buttered leeks, in raspberry and almond tartlets, and in the well-known Irish potato dishes, champ and colcannon.

Darina's brother, Rory O'Connell, who assisted her during the television programmes, cooked at Ballymaloe for many years. He now has his own interior design business. On her first day as Ballymaloe's first outside student, and straight from hotel school, Darina met Myrtle's eldest son whom she married some two years later. She now runs the renowned Ballymaloe cookery school, and loves every minute of teaching, passing on the secrets, as well as taking away the mystique, of good cooking.

---

*Darina Allen with, from left: Ballymaloe Brown
Yeast Bread (page 34), Spotted Dog (page 35),
Sweet White Scones served with Home-made Raspberry
Jam (page 33), Fresh Berry and Almond Tart (page 29)
and Ballymaloe Praline Ice Cream (page 30).*

❧ *Connemara Broth* ❧

Serves 4 – 6

2 tablespoons olive oil (or
    sunflower oil)
150 g (5 oz) piece rindless green
    streaky bacon, cut into
    6 mm (1¼ in) dice and
    blanched
150 g (5 oz) potatoes, cut into
    6 mm (1¼ in) dice
50 g (2 oz) onions, chopped
1 small clove garlic, crushed
    (optional)

900 ml (1½ pints) home-made
    chicken stock
175 g (6 oz) tomatoes, peeled
    and chopped (or the same
    weight tinned tomatoes)
½ teaspoon sugar
salt and freshly ground black
    pepper
25 g (1 oz) Savoy cabbage,
    chopped

TO SERVE
chopped parsley, to garnish

Heat the oil in a large saucepan and fry the bacon in it until the fat runs and
the bacon is crisp and golden. Add the potatoes and onions, and garlic if
using. Cover with a piece of greaseproof paper and then a lid and sweat
over gentle heat for 10 minutes. Add the chicken stock and tomatoes and
season well with the sugar and black pepper. Bring to the boil, then reduce
the heat and simmer for 5 minutes. Add the cabbage and continue to simmer
just until the cabbage is cooked. Taste and adjust the seasoning.

Sprinkle with chopped parsley and serve.

❧ *Potato and Fresh Herb Soup* ❧

Serves 4 – 6

50 g (2 oz) butter
100 g (4 oz) onions, chopped
675 g (1¼ lb) potatoes, diced
about 3 tablespoons chopped
    herbs – choose from
    thyme, parsley, rosemary,
    tarragon and lemon balm

TO SERVE
chopped herbs, to garnish

salt and freshly ground black
    pepper
about 900 ml (1½ pints) home-
    made chicken stock
about 300 ml (10 fl oz) creamy
    milk

Melt the butter in a large saucepan and add the onions and potatoes. Stir well until the vegetables are coated with butter, then add the herbs and season generously with salt and black pepper. Cover with a round of greaseproof paper and then a lid and sweat over gentle heat for 10 minutes. Add the chicken stock and milk and bring to the boil, then reduce the heat and simmer, covered, for about 15 minutes until the potatoes are tender. Cool slightly then liquidise in a food processor. Adjust the thickness of the soup with extra stock or milk if necessary, then re-heat and adjust seasoning if necessary.

Serve sprinkled with chopped herbs.

🌸 Green Lettuce and 🌸 Mint Soup

Serves 4 – 6

50 g (2 oz) butter
100 g (4 oz) onions, chopped
150 g (5 oz) potatoes, diced
salt and freshly ground black
   pepper

1 litre (1¾ pints) home-made
   chicken stock
225 g (8 oz) lettuce, shredded
   (stalks removed)
3 tablespoons chopped mint

TO SERVE
thick cream
chopped mint, to garnish

Melt the butter in a large saucepan and add the onions and potatoes. Stir well until the vegetables are coated with butter. Season generously with salt and black pepper. Cover with a piece of greaseproof paper and then a lid and sweat over gentle heat for 10 minutes. Add the chicken stock and bring to the boil, then reduce the heat and simmer, covered, for about 15 minutes until the potatoes are tender. Stir in the lettuce and mint and bring back to the boil. Cook for 1 minute only. Cool slightly, then liquidise in a food processor. Re-heat and adjust seasoning if necessary.

Serve with a dollop of thick cream and a sprinkling of chopped mint.

❧ Baked Sole ❧
Cucumber Hollandaise Sauce

Serves 4

4 × 450 – 750 g (1 – 1½ lb) fresh
    lemon or Dover sole (or
    plaice)
salt and freshly ground black
    pepper

TO SERVE
Cucumber Hollandaise Sauce
    (below)

Pre-heat the oven to gas mark 5, 375°F (190°C).

Wash the fish and clean the slit below their heads very thoroughly. Remove and discard the heads. With a very sharp knife cut through the dark skin, down both sides of the fish just inside the frill. Make sure to cut right through the skin and to cross the side cuts at the tail.

Lay the fish in a shallow baking tin in 5 mm (¼ in) water. Season generously with salt and black pepper. Bake in the oven for 15 – 20 minutes. The fish are cooked when they feel firm to the touch and when their flesh is white and lifts easily off the bone. The water should have just evaporated when the fish are cooked.

To serve, peel the skin off the fish and transfer them to warmed plates. Spoon over the Cucumber Hollandaise Sauce and serve immediately.

Cucumber Hollandaise Sauce

115 g (4½ oz) butter, diced
100 g (4 oz) peeled, de-seeded
    cucumber, diced
2 egg yolks

1 teaspoon lemon juice
salt and freshly ground black
    pepper

Melt 15 g (½ oz) of the butter in a small saucepan and sauté the cucumber in it until just tender. Remove from the saucepan and set aside. Put the egg yolks in a heavy-based saucepan and add 2 teaspoons cold water. Whisk continuously over very gentle heat until slightly thickened. Add the remaining butter a little at a time, whisking continuously. As soon as one piece melts, add the next. The mixture will gradually thicken. If it shows signs of becoming too thick, or scrambling slightly, immediately remove it from the heat and add a little cold water. Do not leave the saucepan or stop whisking until the sauce is thick enough to coat the back of a wooden spoon. Finally, add the lemon juice and salt and black pepper to taste. If the sauce is too thick add a little warm water. Stir in the cucumber and pour the sauce into a bowl. Keep warm over hot, but not boiling, water.

🍂 *Baked Plaice* 🍂
Fresh Herb Butter

Serves 2

2 × 450 – 700 g (1 – 1½ lb) fresh
    plaice (or lemon sole)
salt and freshly ground black
    pepper

TO SERVE
Fresh Herb Butter (below)

Pre-heat the oven to gas mark 5, 375°F (190°C).

Wash the fish and clean the slit below their heads very thoroughly. Remove and discard the heads. With a very sharp knife cut through the dark skin, down both sides of the fish just inside the frill. Make sure to cut right through the skin and to cross the side cuts at the tail.

Lay the fish in a shallow baking tin in 5 mm (¼ in) water. Season generously with salt and black pepper. Bake in the oven for 15 – 20 minutes. The fish are cooked when they feel firm to the touch and when their flesh is white and lifts easily off the bone. The water should have just evaporated when the fish are cooked.

To serve, peel the skin off the fish and transfer them to warmed plates. Spoon over the Herb Butter and serve immediately.

Fresh Herb Butter
50 g (2 oz) butter
4 teaspoons finely chopped
    mixed herbs such as
    parsley, chives, fennel and
    thyme

Melt the butter in a small saucepan and stir in the herbs.

❧ *Poached Mackerel* ❧
Bretonne Sauce

Serves 4

4 very fresh mackerel
1 teaspoon salt

TO SERVE
Bretonne Sauce (below)
buttered leeks
boiled new potatoes (optional)

Cut the heads off the mackerel, then gut and clean them keeping the fish whole. Bring 1.2 litres (2 pints) water to the boil in an oval casserole and add the salt. Set the mackerel in the water, which must cover the mackerel. If it doesn't, add more boiling water with salt added in the proportions above. Bring back to the boil, then cover with a lid and remove from the heat. After 8 – 10 minutes, check to see whether the mackerel are cooked. The flesh should feel firm to the touch and lift easily off the bone.

To serve, transfer the mackerel to a plate, peel off the skin and carefully lift the fillets off the bones and on to warmed plates. Coat carefully with warm Bretonne Sauce. Serve with buttered leeks and perhaps some new potatoes.

Bretonne Sauce

2 egg yolks (preferably free-range)
1 teaspoon French mustard – we use Maille mustard with green herbs
2 tablespoons finely chopped, mixed herbs such as chives, fennel, parsley and thyme
100 g (4 oz) butter
salt and freshly ground black pepper

Whisk the egg yolks in a bowl with the mustard and herbs. Melt the butter in a small saucepan and bring to the boil, then pour it in a steady stream on to the egg yolks, whisking continuously until the sauce is thick enough to lightly coat the back of a wooden spoon. Season with salt and black pepper. Keep the sauce warm in a pottery or plastic bowl (not stainless steel) in a saucepan of hot, but not boiling, water.

steam until tender. Drain and leave to cool slightly. Cover the spring onions with the milk and bring slowly to the boil. Simmer for about 3 – 4 minutes, then turn off the heat and leave to infuse.

Peel and mash the potatoes and, while hot, mix with the milk and onions. Beat in half of the butter and season to taste with salt and black pepper.

Serve with the rest of the butter melting in the centre.

In Ulster, freshly cooked peas are sometimes added to the champ. Use about 100 g (4 oz).

Colcannon

Follow the recipe for Champ, but replace the spring onions with 225 g (8 oz) freshly cooked, chopped cabbage, leeks or nettles.

🌸 *Potato Cakes* 🌸

Makes 6 wedges

750 g (1½ lb) potatoes
a pinch of salt
1 tablespoon plain flour
½ egg, beaten

1 tablespoon chopped mixed
 herbs such as parsley, thyme
 and chives (optional)
salt and freshly ground black
 pepper
butter for frying

Scrub the potatoes and place them in a saucepan of cold water. Add a good pinch of salt and bring to the boil. Cook for about 20 minutes, then drain off most of the water and allow the potatoes to finish cooking in their own steam until tender. Drain and leave to cool slightly.

Peel and mash the potatoes and, while hot, combine them with the flour, egg, herbs if wished, and plenty of salt and black pepper. Turn the potato mixture on to a floured surface and shape into a large round about 2 cm (¾ in) thick. Cut into 6 wedges.

Fry the wedges slowly in plenty of butter for about 5 minutes on each side until crisp and golden-brown. Serve immediately.

Place the egg yolks in a large bowl and whisk until light and fluffy. Combine the caster sugar with 250 ml (8 fl oz) water in a small heavy-based saucepan and heat gently until the sugar is completely dissolved. Boil the syrup to 110°C (230°F) on a sugar thermometer – it should form a thread if a little is dropped from a spoon into cold water. Immediately, pour the syrup in a steady stream onto the egg yolks, whisking all the time. Continue to whisk until the mixture becomes a thick, creamy white mousse, then stir in the vanilla essence. Fold in the cream, then pour into a clean container, cover and freeze.

Meanwhile, make the praline. Place the almonds and sugar in a heavy-based saucepan over low heat until the sugar dissolves and turns a rich caramel colour. Carefully rotate the saucepan until the almonds just begin to pop and are covered with caramel. Pour the caramel mixture on to a lightly oiled Swiss roll tin or marble slab. Allow to cool and go hard. Crush in a food processor or with a rolling pin. The texture should be quite coarse and gritty.

When the ice cream is just beginning to set, after 2 – 3 hours, fold in half of the praline and freeze again until firm.

To serve, scoop the ice cream in balls and, if you wish, pile into an ice bowl. Sprinkle with the remaining praline.

Ballymaloe Ice Bowl

Take 2 bowls, one about double the size of the other. Half-fill the larger bowl with water and float the second bowl inside it. Weigh the second bowl down with water or ice cubes until the rims of both bowls are level. Place a square of fabric on top of the bowls and secure it with a strong rubber band, or string, just under the rim of the larger bowl. Adjust the smaller bowl until it is in a central position. Place the bowls on a Swiss roll tin in the freezer.

After 24 hours, take the bowls out of the freezer and remove the cloth. Set aside for 15 – 20 minutes, then remove the small bowl. Carefully remove the ice bowl that will have formed between the 2 bowls. Fill the ice bowl with scoops of ice cream and return to the freezer until needed.

To serve, place the ice bowl on a large plate with a folded napkin underneath to catch the drips, and surround with flowers or leaves.

❧ *Marzipan Apples* ❧

Serves 6

Marzipan (below)
6 medium-size dessert apples,
　such as Worcester
　Pearmain, Golden Delicious
　or Cox's Orange Pippin

100 g (4 oz) caster sugar
2 teaspoons ground cinnamon
50 g (2 oz) melted butter

TO SERVE
softly whipped cream

First make the marzipan, then pre-heat the oven to gas mark 4, 350°F (180°C).

Peel and core the apples. Stuff the cavities with the marzipan filling. Mix the caster sugar with the ground cinnamon and roll the apples first in the melted butter and then in the sugar and cinnamon mixture. Place the apples in an ovenproof dish and bake in the oven for 50–60 minutes until very tender.

Serve warm with a bowl of softly whipped cream.

MARZIPAN
225 g (8 oz) sugar
1 egg white
175 g (6 oz) ground almonds
1 drop only of natural almond
　essence (optional)

Dissolve the sugar in 65 ml (2½ fl oz) water in a saucepan over gentle heat, then bring to the boil. Cook to 240°F (116°C) on a sugar thermometer — a teaspoonful of the syrup should immediately form a soft ball if it is dropped into a saucer of cold water. Keep the sides of the saucepan brushed down with water to prevent any crystallisation of sugar.

Remove the syrup from the heat and stir until cloudy. Lightly beat the egg white, then add the ground almonds, egg white, and almond essence if using to the syrup. Mix very well to form a firm paste. Turn the mixture into a bowl and allow to become cool and firm. (Marzipan will keep for 3–4 weeks in a refrigerator.)

❧ *Spotted Dog* ❧

This traditional Irish sweet cake is called Spotted Dog, Currie Cake, Spotted Dick or Railway Cake depending on the area.

450 g (1 lb) plain flour	75 – 100 g (3 – 4 oz) sultanas,
2 teaspoons sugar	raisins or currants
1 teaspoon salt	300 – 400 ml (10 – 14 fl oz)
1 teaspoon bicarbonate of	buttermilk
soda	1 egg, beaten (optional)

Pre-heat the oven to gas mark 8, 450°F (230°C).

Sift the flour, sugar, salt and bicarbonate of soda into a large bowl. Add the dried fruit and mix well. Make a well in the centre of the bowl and pour in most of the buttermilk, and the egg if using. Using one hand, mix in the flour from the sides of the bowl, adding more buttermilk if necessary until the dough comes together. It should be soft, but not too wet and sticky.

Turn the dough out on to a floured board and knead lightly for a few seconds to neaten the shape. Pat into a large round about 4 cm (1½ in) deep and cut a deep cross on the top to extend over the sides of the bread. Place on a lightly floured baking tray and bake for 15 minutes, then reduce the temperature to gas mark 6, 400°F (200°C) and bake for a further 30 minutes, or until the loaf sounds hollow when you tap its base. Cool on a wire tray and serve fresh with plenty of butter.

❧ *Caramelised Walnuts* ❧

Makes 40

40 walnut halves
75 g (3 oz) Marzipan (see p. 32)
200 g (7 oz) sugar

Sandwich the walnut halves together with the marzipan.

In a saucepan, dissolve the sugar in 120 ml (4 fl oz) water over gentle heat, then cook to a rich caramel colour. Dip the walnuts into the caramel, one at a time. Shake off excess caramel. Allow to harden on a lightly oiled baking tray.

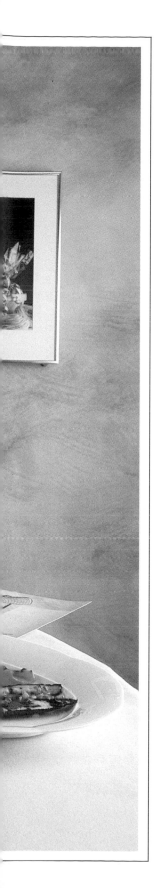

Antonio Carluccio

ANTONIO CARLUCCIO GREW UP in northern Italy, and his cooking stems from memories of the idyllic village in which he spent his earliest years. In the heart of truffle and mushroom country, it presented him with all the ingredients to nurture a love of nature and of good food. Later, when dealing in Italian wines in northern Europe, he taught himself to cook the dishes of his homeland and of his own region, learning from books and through trial and error. As he says, there are not many ways of cooking good basic ingredients.

If food in general is his passion, the study and collection of wild mushrooms is a passionate hobby. He has been enthusing the British about both, ever since he came to London in 1975, through his books, television programmes and the dishes served in his bustling *Neal Street Restaurant*. Funghi are indisputably the speciality of the house, and may be offered in a rabbit stew, a soup, with pasta or polenta, or in a risotto – his favourite dish, made with vialone nano rice and spiked with cubes of Parma ham, fresh and dried porcini, freshly grated Parmesan and the thinnest shavings of white truffle. Food in his restaurant is the quintessence of Italy and Carluccio: 'Good flavour above all, good ingredients, very little cooking time and no messing around. That's me.'

Antonio Carluccio with, from left: Stinging Nettle Gnocchi with Tomato and Cheese Sauce (page 40), Venison Carpaccio (page 47) and Italian Antipasto (page 38).

❧ *Italian Antipasto* ❧
(Grilled Vegetables with Mint and Olive Oil)

Serves 4

4 long slices aubergine, approx.
    1 cm (⅜ in) thick
4 long slices courgettes, approx.
    1 cm (⅜ in) thick

2 large yellow peppers,
    de-seeded and quartered
1 tablespoon olive oil

TO SERVE
Vinaigrette (below)
1 tablespoon coarsely chopped
    mint

1 tablespoon coarsely chopped
    flat-leaf parsley
Bagna Cauda (below)

Pre-heat the oven to gas mark 8, 450°F (230°C).

Pre-heat the grill to high. Grill the slices of aubergine and courgette, without oil, for 2½ minutes on each side until soft. Put the quartered peppers on an oiled baking tray and sprinkle with the olive oil. Bake in the oven for about 20 minutes, until the tips of the peppers are starting to go brown and charred.

Sprinkle the vinaigrette over the aubergine and courgette slices. Sprinkle the mint over the aubergines and the parsley over the courgettes. Fill the pepper quarters with a little of the Bagna Cauda. Serve with some good bread.

Vinaigrette
8 tablespoons virgin olive oil
2 tablespoons balsamic vinegar
1 clove garlic, finely chopped

Mix together the olive oil, balsamic vinegar and garlic.

Bagna Cauda
4 cloves garlic
120 ml (4 fl oz) milk
15 g (½ oz) butter
10 anchovy fillets in oil, drained

Put the garlic in a saucepan with the milk and cook gently until soft. This will take about 35 minutes. Throw away most of the milk, then add the butter and the anchovies. Let the mixture slowly dissolve over a low heat until a paste is produced. Pass through a sieve.

❧ *Endive and Borlotti Bean Soup* ❧

Serves 4

100 g (4 oz) dried borlotti beans
(or 1 × 432 g/15 oz tin
borlotti beans)
salt
350 g (12 oz) curly endive
6 tablespoons olive oil
100 g (4 oz) speck (or smoked
bacon), cut into cubes
4 cloves garlic, sliced
¼ – 2 red chillies, sliced

Put the dried borlotti beans to soak for 12 hours or more in a large bowl. Drain, then boil for 2 hours in fresh unsalted water. Add salt at the end of cooking time. If you are using canned beans, drain and wash them before use.

Wash the endive and cut into short lengths. Heat the olive oil in a large saucepan. Fry the speck cubes until crispy, then add the garlic and cook gently without letting it brown. Add the endive, and chilli to taste. Over high heat, stir-fry for a minute or two, coating the endive with the oil. Add the drained borlotti beans, some salt and about 600 ml (1 pint) water. If you are using canned beans, they will absorb less liquid, so reduce the amount of water to about 300 ml (10 fl oz), adding more as required.

Bring to the boil, then reduce the heat and simmer until the endive and beans are tender and most of the liquid has evaporated. The consistency should be slightly soupy.

❧ *Lobster Spaghettini* ❧

Serves 4

1 lobster (approx.
    1.25 kg/2½ lb), freshly
    cooked for 12–15 minutes
4 tablespoons olive oil
2 cloves garlic, thinly sliced
1 dried, hot red chilli, sliced
½ glass white wine

6 tablespoons passata di
    pomodoro
350–400 g (12–14 oz) fresh
    spaghettini
2 tablespoons chopped parsley
generous quantity of freshly
    ground black pepper

Remove all the meat from the lobster's body and claws and cut in small pieces. Reserve any juices. Heat the olive oil in a large, heavy saucepan, then add the garlic and fry for about 1 minute taking care that the garlic does not brown. Add the chilli, then add the white wine and allow it to bubble for 1 minute. Stir in the passata di pomodoro and reserved lobster juices and simmer gently for 10 minutes. Stir in the lobster pieces.

Cook the spaghettini in plenty of boiling, salted water until al dente. Drain and mix with the sauce and parsley.

Serve in warm dishes with plenty of freshly ground black pepper.

❧ *Stinging Nettle Gnocchi* ❧
Tomato and Cheese Sauce

Serves 4

100 g (4 oz) young stinging nettle
    tops, leaves only
1 egg

450 g (1 lb) floury potatoes,
    cooked, drained and
    mashed
100 g (4 oz) plain flour
a pinch of salt

TO SERVE
Tomato and Cheese Sauce
    (opposite)
50 g (2 oz) Parmesan cheese,
    freshly grated

Cook the stinging nettles in boiling, salted water for 2 minutes. Drain, squeeze out excess moisture and chop finely. Blend the nettles in a food processor with the egg for a few seconds.

Mix the mashed potatoes with the flour. Add the nettles and mix well to obtain a semi-soft dough. With floured hands, roll the mixture into long 'sausages'. Cut into 2.5 cm (1 in) pieces.

Boil a large saucepan of water with 10 g (¼ oz) salt per litre (1¾ pints) water. Make the Tomato and Cheese Sauce while the water is coming to a boil.

Plunge the gnocchi into the boiling water. They will be cooked within about 20–30 seconds, when they rise to the surface. Remove them from the saucepan with a draining spoon and drain thoroughly.

To serve, add the gnocchi to the sauce and mix well. Serve on individual plates sprinkled with the Parmesan cheese.

Tomato and Cheese Sauce
1 × 400 g (14 oz) tin chopped
      tomatoes
6 tablespoons mascarpone
      cheese
175 g (6 oz) dolcelatte cheese,
      cut into small pieces

Put the chopped tomatoes in a saucepan and heat through thoroughly. Add the mascarpone and dolcelatte and, on a very low heat, reduce the mixture to a cream, stirring gently.

Baked Polenta with Funghi

Serves 4

350 g (12 oz) fresh ceps (or
      button mushrooms) plus
   25 g (1 oz) dried ceps
      (porcini)
1 small onion, chopped
3 tablespoons olive oil
25 g (1 oz) unsalted butter

1 × 400 g (14 oz) tin chopped
      plum tomatoes
salt and freshly ground black
      pepper
350 g (12 oz) fontina cheese,
      sliced
50 g (2 oz) Parmesan cheese,
      freshly grated

POLENTA
175 g (6 oz) yellow polenta flour
      (or ½ × 370 g/13 oz pack
      Valsugana or Star polenta)

25 g (1 oz) butter
50 g (2 oz) Parmesan cheese,
      freshly grated

For the sauce, clean and slice the fresh mushrooms. Soak the dried ceps for 10 minutes in lukewarm water, then drain. Fry the onion in the oil and butter, then add the sliced fresh mushrooms. Cook over a high heat for 10 minutes, then add the tomatoes and the drained ceps. Continue cooking for another 20 minutes so that the liquid from the tomatoes evaporates. Season to taste with salt and black pepper.

For the polenta, bring 750 ml (1¼ pints) salted water to the boil. Very carefully add the polenta flour, stirring constantly to prevent lumps from forming. Continue to stir the polenta until it starts to come away from the sides of the saucepan – 30 minutes if you are using ordinary polenta flour, 5 minutes for Valsugana or Star polenta. Stir in the butter and Parmesan cheese

At this point you have two alternatives. The first is to pour the 'wet' polenta on to plates and serve with the hot sauce, sprinkled with the Parmesan cheese.

For the second alternative, pre-heat the oven to gas mark 7, 425°F (220°C). Spread the polenta in a flat container, leave until cold and then cut into sticks. Make alternate layers of the polenta, fontina cheese and sauce in an ovenproof dish. Finish with a layer of sauce and the Parmesan cheese. Bake for about 30 minutes until bubbling and golden.

❦ *Tagliatelle with Radicchio* ❦ *and Rocket*

Serves 4

4 tablespoons olive oil
1 medium-size red onion, chopped
100 g (4 oz) thickly cut speck, cut into small strips
2 tablespoons dry red wine
150 g (5 oz) radicchio, finely sliced

450 g (1 lb) fresh tagliatelle (or 300–350 g/10–12 oz dry tagliatelle)
100 g (4 oz) rocket, roughly chopped
salt and freshly ground black pepper

Heat the olive oil in a saucepan or frying-pan and gently fry the onion and speck in it until the onion is soft. Add the wine and allow to evaporate a little, then add the radicchio and allow it to soften. Season with salt and black pepper.

Cook the tagliatelle in plenty of boiling, salted water until it is al dente, then drain thoroughly. Mix with the sauce.

Serve each portion with a sprinkling of rocket.

🌺 *Risotto with Parma Ham* 🌺 *and Truffles*

Serves 4

15 g (½ oz) dried ceps (porcini), soaked in cold water for 30 minutes

1.2–1.5 litres (2–2½ pints) hot chicken stock

1 small onion, finely chopped

75 g (3 oz) unsalted butter

50 g (2 oz) Parma ham, cubed

350 g (12 oz) vialone nano or carnaroli rice

salt and freshly ground black pepper

50 g (2 oz) Parmesan cheese, freshly grated

about 40 g (1½ oz) fresh white truffle, thinly sliced, to garnish (optional)

Drain and chop the ceps. Add the soaking liquid to the chicken stock. In a large saucepan, lightly fry the finely chopped onion in half of the butter. When this is half cooked, add the Parma ham and the drained, chopped ceps and fry for 2–3 minutes. Add the rice and stir well until all the rice grains are covered with butter. Pour in a ladleful of hot stock and continue cooking until the liquid is absorbed. Gradually add more stock, a ladleful at a time, and continue until the rice absorbs all the liquid. This will take about 20–25 minutes. The rice should be tender and the risotto should be fairly moist. Season to taste with salt and black pepper and stir in the remaining butter with the Parmesan cheese. Mix well. Serve on hot dishes. Garnish with slices of fresh white truffle, if wished.

❧ *Semolina Gnocchi* ❧ *with Herbs*

Serves 4–6

500 ml (18 fl oz) milk
½ teaspoon salt and freshly
    ground black pepper to taste
4 grates of nutmeg
225 g (8 oz) coarse semolina
    flour
1 egg plus 1 egg yolk, beaten

2 tablespoons coarsely chopped
    parsley
1 tablespoon finely chopped
    basil
1 teaspoon finely chopped
    rosemary
65 g (2½ oz) unsalted butter
75 g (3 oz) Parmesan cheese,
    freshly grated

Heat the milk together with the salt, black pepper and nutmeg. When it begins to boil add the semolina flour little by little, stirring all the time with a whisk to prevent lumps from forming. Once all the semolina is incorporated, leave the mixture to simmer for about 20 minutes over a very low heat stirring from time to time. Remove the pan from the heat. When the semolina is cool, thoroughly stir in the beaten egg and herbs. Spread the mixture on a working surface – preferably marble – to a thickness of 2 cm (¾ in). Leave until firm.

Pre-heat the oven to gas mark 7, 425°F (220°C).

Using a 5 cm (2 in) diameter glass or pastry cutter, cut out rounds of gnocchi. These can be stored in the refrigerator if you are not using them immediately. Arrange the gnocchi, one overlapping the other, in a well-buttered ovenproof dish. Dot the gnocchi with little pieces of butter and sprinkle with half of the Parmesan cheese. Bake in the oven until the tips of the gnocchi begin to brown. This will take about 20 minutes. Sprinkle with the remaining Parmesan cheese and serve immediately.

*Antonio Carluccio's Risotto with Parma Ham
and Truffles (page 43).*

❧ Mixed Marinated Fish ❧

Serves 2

4 fresh sardines, cleaned
4 small mackerel, cleaned and
   heads removed

4 small trout, cleaned and heads
   removed
plain flour for dusting
corn oil for frying

MARINADE

8 tablespoons olive oil
1 medium-size red onion, sliced
1 medium-size white onion,
   sliced
3 cloves garlic, sliced
1 tablespoon white sugar

2 wine glasses white wine
   vinegar
1 glass white wine
4 bay leaves
1 sprig of rosemary
1 tablespoon black peppercorns
a pinch of salt

Wash the fish and thoroughly dry them with a cloth. Dust in the flour so that they are evenly coated on all sides. Heat the oil in a large frying-pan and fry the fish in it over medium heat until they are crisp and golden on each side. Remove from the frying-pan and drain on kitchen paper.

For the marinade, heat the olive oil in a saucepan and fry the onions until transparent. Add the garlic and cook for 2–3 minutes, stirring to prevent it browning. Add the sugar, vinegar, wine, bay leaves, rosemary, peppercorns and salt. Bring to the boil and simmer for 20 minutes.

Lay the fried fish side-by-side in a shallow, earthenware dish. Pour the hot marinade over and leave for at least 12–24 hours in a cool place or in the refrigerator. Turn the fish while they marinate. Serve at room temperature.

❧ Baked Savoy Cabbage ❧

Serves 4

2 cloves garlic, sliced
4 tablespoons olive oil
750 g (1½ lb) Savoy cabbage,
  shredded
1 litre (1¾ pints) chicken stock
a good pinch of salt
a dash of nutmeg

6 thick slices ciabatta bread
100 g (4 oz) unsalted butter
10 anchovy fillets (optional)
65 g (2½ oz) Parmesan cheese,
  freshly grated
200 g (7 oz) fontina cheese,
  thinly sliced

Pre-heat the oven to gas mark 6, 400°F (200°C).

Gently fry the garlic in the olive oil but do not let it brown. Add the cabbage, three-quarters of the stock and the salt and nutmeg. Cook for 20 minutes until the cabbage is tender, stirring from time to time. Meanwhile, fry the bread in the butter until golden-brown. Each slice will absorb quite a lot of butter.

Place 3 slices of fried bread in an ovenproof dish. Cover with a layer of half of the cabbage, half of the anchovies, some grated Parmesan cheese and some slices of fontina cheese. Pour over some of the remaining stock and repeat the layers of bread and cabbage, anchovies and cheese. Add enough stock to keep the mixture moist. Finish with a layer of fontina and Parmesan. Bake in the oven for 25 minutes until bubbling and golden.

❧ Asparagus with Speck ❧

Serves 4

500–750 g (1¼–1½ lb) tender
  green asparagus
500 g (1¼ lb) new potatoes,
  scraped or scrubbed

200 g (7 oz) speck, sliced
50 g (2 oz) unsalted butter,
  melted
freshly ground black pepper

Peel and trim the asparagus stalks, keeping only the green parts. Cook the asparagus whole in slightly salted water until tender. This will take about 8 minutes if the asparagus are large. Boil the new potatoes for 15–20 minutes until tender.

Arrange the slices of speck on one large serving plate or 4 individual ones. Lay the asparagus and potatoes beside the speck, and spoon melted butter over them. Sprinkle with black pepper.

🥀 *Hazelnut Cake* 🥀

Serves 8

125 g (4½ oz) hazelnuts
100 g (4 oz) unsalted butter,
    softened plus butter for
    greasing
125 g (4½ oz) caster sugar
4 large eggs, separated
25 g (1 oz) plain flour, sifted
125 g (4½ oz) ricotta cheese
1 teaspoon grated lemon rind
6 tablespoons apricot jam
25 g (1 oz) bitter chocolate,
    grated

Pre-heat the oven to gas mark 6, 400°F (200°C).

Lay the hazelnuts on a baking tray and roast them for 10–15 minutes until light golden. Rub off the skins, allow the hazelnuts to cool and grind coarsely. You will need to reduce the oven temperature to gas mark 5, 375°F (190°C) to bake the cake.

Butter a 25 cm (10 in) loose-bottom flat tin.

Cream the butter, add two-thirds of the caster sugar and beat well. Beat in the egg yolks and continue to beat until the mixture is soft and foamy. Fold in the flour. In a separate bowl, beat the ricotta with a fork until it is light, then add the coarsely ground hazelnuts and the grated lemon rind. Add this to the egg yolk and flour. Beat the egg whites until stiff and fold in the remaining caster sugar. Very carefully, fold the ricotta, egg and flour mixture into the beaten egg whites. Spread into the flan tin and bake for 25–30 minutes until golden and just firm to the touch.

Let the cake cool a little, then remove from the flan tin and unmould on to a plate. Mix the apricot jam with a little water and spread it evenly over the top of the cake. Sprinkle with grated chocolate.

A glass of Passito di Caluso dessert wine is the ideal accompaniment – if you can find it!

❧ *Tiramisu* ❧

Serves 6—8

1 egg yolk
1 teaspoon vanilla sugar
250 g (9 oz) mascarpone cheese
2 tablespoons single cream
150 ml (5 fl oz) strong black
 coffee
1 tablespoon kahlua
12 Savoiardi biscuits (sponge
 fingers)
12 Amaretti biscuits
85—120 ml (3—4 fl oz) Moscato
 Passito (or sherry)
250 ml (8 fl oz) double cream,
 lightly whipped
1 tablespoon cocoa powder

Put the egg yolk and vanilla sugar in a bowl and mix gently to a cream consistency. Beat in the mascarpone cheese and single cream. Mix the coffee and kahlua. Briefly dip the Savoiardi into the coffee-kahlua liquid and place on the base of a large bowl. Cover with a layer of the mascarpone mixture. Dip the Amaretti biscuits in the Moscato Passito and use them to cover the mascarpone. Finally, make a top layer with the double cream.

Sprinkle with the cocoa powder and chill in the refrigerator until set.

Anton Edelmann

ANTON EDELMANN CANNOT CLAIM always to have liked cooking, but he has certainly always liked eating. From his early teens, he helped in the kitchens of his uncle's restaurant in Bavaria during school holidays, and enjoyed the company of his co-workers, the atmosphere, the hustle and bustle and, above all, the end result. His love of actual cooking came later as he gradually became better at it. After a basic training, and experience in kitchens such as The Dorchester and 90 Park Lane, he found his home in the *River Room* at that London institution, the Savoy Hotel.

The Edelmann style is classical, but he prefers to define it as good food, honestly cooked. However, it is far from plain, for he believes that sophisticated cooking should always emerge from simple beginnings. The French influence is strong, but there are nods towards the country in which he is working and living. His soup of fish from the Atlantic, Britain's answer to bouillabaisse, is one example; another is black pudding with calves liver. There are also oriental influences, and a reinterpretation of that American standard, the burger. Another strand of his style is vegetarian. For some six years he has been creating imaginative dishes in his *menu de régime naturel*.

Anton Edelmann with, clockwise from left: Fig Tart
with Raspberry Coulis (page 67), Rouille (page 55),
North Atlantic Fish Soup (page 54), Rosettes of Lamb
in Roestis with Vegetables and Wine Sauce (page 63).

North Atlantic Fish Soup

Serves 4

1 small lobster
1 kg (2 lb) mussels
½ clove garlic
200 g (7 oz) white mirepoix
  (chopped onion, white of
  leek and celery)
200 ml (7 fl oz) dry white wine
600 ml (1 pint) strong chicken
  stock (or fish stock)
40 g (1½ oz) fennel, finely diced
40 g (1½ oz) carrot, finely diced
50 g (2 oz) leek, finely diced
2 tablespoons olive oil
a generous pinch of saffron
  threads

100 g (4 oz) salmon fillet, cut
  into 4 strips
100 g (4 oz) white fish fillet such
  as turbot or brill, cut into
  4 strips
4 scallops, roes removed, cut in
  half crossways
25 g (1 oz) vermicelli, boiled in
  salted water until al dente
50 g (2 oz) plum tomatoes,
  peeled, de-seeded and finely
  diced
cayenne pepper
salt and freshly ground black
  pepper

TO SERVE
1 teaspoon chopped fennel herb
wafer-thin slices baguette, toasted
Rouille (opposite)

Boil the lobster for 6 minutes, then shell its tail and claws. Cut the tail meat into 6 medallions. Thoroughly wash and scrub the mussels under cold, running water. Ensure that they are all firmly closed. Place in a saucepan with the garlic, mirepoix, white wine and about 150 ml (5 fl oz) of the stock. Cover, and cook over high heat for 3–5 minutes, shaking frequently until all the mussels have opened. Discard any that remain closed. Strain the mussels through a colander and reserve the liquid. Place the mussel stock in a tall container tilted at a slight angle to allow any sand or grit to settle. Remove the mussels from their shells, then carefully peel away the brown frill (beard) around each one. Cover the mussels with a damp cloth.

In a saucepan, sweat the fennel, carrot and leek in the oil for about 2 minutes, then add the remaining chicken stock. Carefully ladle off the mussel stock from the top of the container and add to the pan with the saffron. Simmer gently for about 10 minutes until the vegetables are just tender. Season the salmon and white fish with salt and black pepper and add to the stock. Cook for 30 seconds. Add the scallops, lobster claws and tail, mussels, vermicelli and tomatoes. Do not allow to boil – simply warm gently. Season to taste with cayenne pepper, salt and black pepper.

To serve, sprinkle with chopped fennel and serve at once with slices of toasted baguette topped with a tiny amount of Rouille.

Rouille

Makes about 150 ml (5 fl oz)

½ green pepper, de-seeded and
finely chopped

½ chilli, de-seeded and finely
chopped

1½ tinned red peppers, well
drained and chopped

1 clove garlic, crushed

a dash of Tabasco

1 tablespoon olive oil

1 tablespoon dry breadcrumbs

salt and freshly ground black
pepper

Simmer the green pepper and chilli in 50 ml (2 fl oz) water for about
10 minutes until very soft. Drain, then purée with the red peppers and garlic,
and Tabasco to taste. Work in the olive oil a drop at a time, then stir in the
breadcrumbs to thicken. Season to taste with salt and black pepper.

🏵 *Salmon and Scallop Rounds* 🏵
Sauce Epice

Serves 4

450–600 g (1–1¼ lb) salmon (or
salmon trout fillet)

4 scallops, roes removed

skin from a side of salmon,
scales removed

1 tablespoon oil plus extra for
grilling

40 g (1½ oz) unsalted butter,
melted

50 g (2 oz) courgettes, cut into
long, fine strips

50 g (2 oz) kohlrabi, cut into
long, fine strips

50 g (2 oz) carrot, cut into long,
fine strips

TO SERVE

50 ml (2 fl oz) crème fraiche

Sauce Epice (see p. 56)

chopped chives, to garnish

Remove any small bones from the fish with tweezers, then cut 8 strips of
salmon the same depth as the scallops. Trim the strips to an even depth in
the centre and taper them at the ends. Each strip should go halfway round
a scallop. Wrap 2 strips of salmon around each scallop to encase it completely.
Cut the salmon skin into 4 strips the depth of the salmon-and-scallop rounds

and wrap a strip around each one. Heat a small, non-stick frying-pan and add 1 tablespoon oil. Seal the salmon skin joins by pressing the join into the hot frying-pan. Season the fish rounds generously with salt and black pepper and brush with 15 g (½ oz) of the melted butter.

Heat a solid grill or heavy-based frying-pan and brush with oil. Set the salmon and scallop rounds on the grill and cook for about 2 minutes each side, until lightly browned and just firm to the touch. Blanch the courgette, kohlrabi and carrot strips in the same saucepan, then drain. Melt the remaining butter and toss this 'vegetable spaghetti' in it until hot. Season to taste.

Just before serving, warm the Sauce Epice and stir in the crème fraiche. Adjust seasoning if necessary.

To serve, arrange a small pile of vegetable spaghetti at the top of each warmed plate. Set a salmon and scallop round beside the vegetables and spoon some Sauce Epice around each portion. Garnish with chopped chives.

Sauce Epice

50 g (2 oz) unsalted butter
150 g (5 oz) onions, finely chopped
1 clove garlic, crushed
150 g (5 oz) red peppers, de-seeded and diced
½ teaspoon curry powder

a generous pinch of saffron threads
salt and freshly ground black pepper
150 g (5 oz) apples, peeled, cored and chopped
450 ml (15 fl oz) fish stock (or chicken stock)

Melt the butter in a saucepan and sweat the onions in it for 8–10 minutes until translucent. Add the garlic and peppers and cook for a further 4 minutes. Stir in the curry powder, saffron, salt and black pepper and cook for 1–2 minutes. Add the apples and stock. Cover and simmer for 20 minutes. Liquidise in a food processor until smooth, then pass through a fine sieve. Adjust seasoning if necessary.

the liver in 2 batches. In the same frying-pan, quickly fry the black pudding slices on both sides.

To serve, spoon some Potato Purée with Garlic into the centre of each warm plate and set 2 slices of liver on top. Arrange an apple round on each portion and top with a slice of black pudding. Spoon some Sauternes Sauce around each portion.

Potato Purée with Garlic

450 g (1 lb) potatoes, peeled and diced
20 g (¾ oz) cloves garlic (about 4 medium-size cloves)
200 ml (7 fl oz) extra virgin olive oil
salt and freshly ground black pepper
75 g (3 oz) leek, diced
120 ml (4 fl oz) double cream
4 tablespoons chopped chives

Place the diced potatoes and garlic in a saucepan with 300 ml (10 fl oz) water. Pour in two thirds of the olive oil and season generously with salt. Bring to the boil, then cook for about 15 minutes until the potatoes are cooked. Drain off any water left in the saucepan.

Blanch the leeks in boiling, salted water until tender, then drain thoroughly. Put to one side. Remove the garlic cloves from the potatoes and crush one of them. Cook it gently in a little of the remaining olive oil. Purée the potatoes, then pass through a sieve.

To serve, beat in the cream, cooked garlic and remaining olive oil, then the leeks and chives. Season to taste with salt and black pepper.

Sauternes Sauce

1 tablespoon olive oil
40 g (1½ oz) onion, finely chopped
2 cloves garlic, crushed
100 ml (3½ fl oz) white wine vinegar
300 ml (10 fl oz) Sauternes
½ teaspoon black peppercorns, crushed
300 ml (10 fl oz) Jus de Veau (see p. 65)
salt and freshly ground black pepper
15 g (½ oz) unsalted butter

Heat the olive oil in a saucepan and sweat the onions and garlic in it for 2–3 minutes until translucent. Add the vinegar, wine and crushed peppercorns and boil rapidly to reduce by three-quarters. This will take about 15 minutes. Add the jus de veau and simmer for 5–10 minutes to a sauce consistency. Season to taste with salt and black pepper. Add the butter and whiz with a hand-held electric blender. Pass through a fine sieve and adjust seasoning if necessary.

🎖 *Provençale Burgers* 🎖

Serves 4

450 g (1 lb) lean leg of pork, minced
onion and garlic mixture, cooled (see Provençale Sauce below)
2 eggs
100 ml (3½ fl oz) double cream

1 tablespoon chopped coriander leaves
salt and freshly ground black pepper
75 g (3 oz) goat's cheese such as Roubiac
4 tablespoons olive oil

TO SERVE
Provençale Sauce (below)

Place the minced pork in a bowl set over another, larger bowl of ice cubes. Beat in the reserved cooled onion and garlic mixture, and then the eggs one at a time. Beat in the cream a little at a time, then add the chopped coriander leaves. Season generously with salt and black pepper.

Cut the goat's cheese into 8 cubes. With wetted hands, take about one-eighth of the pork mixture and shape it into a burger. Press a small cube of cheese into the centre of the burger. Repeat to make 7 more burgers. Heat 2 tablespoons of olive oil in each of 2 non-stick frying-pans and cook the burgers for 5–6 minutes on each side, until golden-brown and firm.

To serve, spoon some of the Provençale Sauce on to each warm plate and set 2 burgers on top.

Provençale Sauce

15 g (½ oz) unsalted butter
1 tablespoon olive oil
150 g (5 oz) onions, finely chopped
2 cloves garlic, crushed
1 tablespoon tomato purée
6 plum tomatoes, peeled, de-seeded and diced – save all the trimmings
300 ml (10 fl oz) chicken stock

salt and freshly ground black pepper
1 teaspoon finely chopped oregano
1 teaspoon finely chopped marjoram
1 teaspoon finely chopped basil
50 g (2 oz) goat's cheese such as Roubiac

In a saucepan, heat the butter with the olive oil and sweat the onions in it until translucent. Add the garlic and cook for a further minute. Remove half the mixture from the saucepan and put to one side to cool. This will be used to make the burgers.

To the onions in the saucepan, add the tomato purée, tomato trimmings and chicken stock. Season to taste with salt and black pepper. Simmer for about 10 minutes until reduced by half. Liquidise in a food processor then pass through a fine sieve. Stir the diced tomato, chopped herbs and goat's cheese into the sauce. Adjust seasoning if necessary and warm gently.

A selection of Anton Edelmann's canapés and frivolities.
From left: Prawns with Sage Leaves (page 69),
Chicken Skewers with Bacon (page 69), Raspberry and
Mango Tartlets (page 71), Cape Gooseberries in Caramel
(page 71), Puff Pastry Hearts and Discs (page 68)
surrounded by Paillettes (page 70).

❀ *Fillets of Pork* ❀
Thai Rice, Thai Curry Sauce

Serves 4

8 × 50 g (2 oz) pieces pork fillet,
    trimmed of all fat and sinew
salt and freshly ground black
    pepper
2 tablespoons vegetable oil
15 g (½ oz) unsalted butter

TO SERVE
Thai Rice (below)
Thai Curry Sauce (opposite)
4 teaspoons flaked almonds,
    toasted
sprigs of coriander, to garnish

Flatten the pieces of pork with the palms of your hands. Tie each one with string to keep a neat shape. Season generously with salt and black pepper. Heat the oil and butter in a frying-pan and fry the pork for 12–15 minutes, until browned and just cooked. Remove the string.

To serve, spoon some Thai Rice into the centre of each warm plate. Set 2 pieces of pork on top and spoon a little Thai Curry Sauce on the meat and some around the rice. Sprinkle with flaked almonds and garnish with sprigs of coriander.

Thai Rice

50 g (2 oz) onion, finely chopped
1 tablespoon vegetable oil
¼ red pepper, de-seeded and
    finely diced
¼ green pepper, de-seeded and
    finely diced

175 g (6 oz) Thai fragrant rice
600 ml (1 pint) chicken stock
a pinch of saffron threads
15 g (½ oz) unsalted butter
salt and freshly ground black
    pepper

In a saucepan, sweat the onion in the oil until translucent, then stir in the diced peppers. Cook for 1 minute. Stir in the rice and stir until it is coated with oil. Add the chicken stock and saffron threads. Cover, and simmer until the rice is tender and the stock is absorbed. This will take about 15 minutes. Stir in the butter and season to taste with salt and black pepper.

Thai Curry Sauce

2 tablespoons vegetable oil
100 g (4 oz) onion, finely
    chopped
2 teaspoons finely chopped red
    chilli
2½ tablespoons finely chopped
    ginger
2 cloves garlic, crushed
¼ teaspoon green peppercorns,
    crushed
1 lemon grass stalk, crushed
½ teaspoon ground coriander
300 ml (10 fl oz) chicken stock
1 × 400 g (14 oz) tin coconut
    milk
salt and freshly ground black
    pepper
lime juice to taste
1 tablespoon chopped coriander
    leaves

Heat the oil in a saucepan and sweat the onion in it for about 2 minutes until translucent. Grind the chilli, ginger, garlic, peppercorns, lemon grass and coriander together and add to the onions. Cook for a further 2 minutes, stirring occasionally. Stir in the chicken stock and coconut milk and bring to the boil. Cook for about 10 minutes, stirring occasionally, until thickened. Cool, then purée and pass through a fine sieve. Season to taste with salt, black pepper and lime juice. Just before serving, warm the sauce and stir in the chopped coriander leaves. Adjust seasoning if necessary.

❧ Rosettes of Lamb in Roestis ❧
Vegetable 'Quenelles', Baby Carrots and Turnips, Wine Sauce

Serves 4

1 very large potato
oil for blanching
salt and freshly ground black
    pepper
2 egg yolks, beaten
8 × 65 g (2½ oz) lamb rosettes
    cut from the best end, all
    skin and fat removed
flour, to dust
15 g (1½ oz) unsalted butter
2 tablespoons olive oil

TO SERVE
Vegetable 'Quenelles' (see p. 64)
Baby Carrots and Turnips (see
    p. 64) and 4 mange tout,
    blanched and halved
    lengthways, to garnish
Wine Sauce (see p. 65)

Square cut the potato on all sides to give a 120 g (4½ oz) piece with straight sides. Cut this into very fine, matchstick-length julienne strips. Blanch the potato strips in warm oil to just soften them. They should stay white and not cook to a golden colour at all. Drain. Season with salt and black pepper, then mix with the egg yolks.

Season the lamb rosettes and lightly dust with flour. Take 1 rosette and some of the potato strips. Starting at the outside edge of the rosette, place a strip of potato on the lamb and curl it round so that it follows the line of the rosette. Set another potato strip where the first one finishes and curl this one round, again following the line of the rosette. Repeat until you have a 'catherine wheel' of potato on top of the meat, completely covering the surface. Repeat this process with the remaining 7 rosettes.

In a frying-pan, fry the rosettes potato-side down in the butter and oil for about 3 minutes until golden. Turn and cook the meat for a further 1–2 minutes. Remove from the frying-pan and keep warm. Do not clean the frying-pan – you will need it for the sauce.

To serve, arrange the Vegetable 'Quenelles' – 1 celeriac and 1 carrot – on each warm plate and set 2 lamb rosettes on each plate. Garnish with Baby Carrots and Turnips and 2 mange tout halves. Pour a little sauce around each portion.

Vegetable 'Quenelles'

450 g (1 lb) celeriac, cubed
350 g (12 oz) carrots, cubed
salt and freshly ground black
    pepper
50 g (2 oz) unsalted butter

Steam the celeriac and carrots separately for 10–15 minutes until tender. Pass through a fine sieve and place each mixture in a saucepan. Dry over heat, then season to taste with salt and black pepper and stir 25 g (1 oz) of the butter into each one. Keep warm.

Baby Carrots and Turnips

12 baby carrots, peeled with a little of the green tops intact
8 baby turnips, peeled with a little of the green tops intact

1 teaspoon unsalted butter
½ teaspoon sugar
salt and freshly ground black pepper

Place the baby vegetables in a saucepan with the butter and sugar. Just cover with water and simmer gently for about 10 minutes until tender and glazed. Season with salt and black pepper and keep warm.

Wine Sauce

about 20 g (¾ oz) unsalted butter
25 g (1 oz) chopped shallot
100 ml (3½ fl oz) dry white wine

200 ml (7 fl oz) Jus de Veau
(below) or good-quality veal
stock
salt and freshly ground black
pepper

Pour off the fat from the frying pan in which the rosettes were fried, and add 1 teaspoon of the butter. Sauté the shallots for 1–2 minutes, then add the white wine and reduce by two-thirds by fast boiling. Add the jus de veau and bring to the boil. Reduce by one-third by fast boiling, then pass through a fine sieve. Season to taste with salt and black pepper. Whisk in the last of the butter.

JUS DE VEAU

Makes about 600 ml (1 pint)
5 pieces veal bone
200 g (7 oz) carrots, roughly
chopped
200 g (7 oz) celery, roughly
chopped
200 g (7 oz) leeks, roughly
chopped
200 g (7 oz) onions, roughly
chopped
1 calf's foot

1 clove garlic, chopped
100 g (4 oz) tomato purée
300 ml (10 fl oz) dry white wine
1 tablespoon black peppercorns,
crushed
a few sprigs of thyme
2 bay leaves
100 g (4 oz) tomato, chopped
salt and freshly ground black
pepper

Place the veal bones in a large saucepan of cold water and bring to the boil. Drain and wash well under cold, running water. Return the bones to the saucepan, add half of the chopped carrots, celery, leeks and onions and cover with cold water. Bring to the boil, then reduce the heat and simmer, covered for 4 hours. Strain and reserve. Discard the bones.

Pre-heat the oven to gas mark 7, 425°F (220°C).

Split the calf's foot in half, place in a roasting tin and roast for about 30 minutes until lightly browned. Add the remaining vegetables and the garlic and tomato purée and roast for a further 15–20 minutes, stirring occasionally.

Transfer to a large saucepan and add the white wine, reserved stock, peppercorns, herbs and tomato trimmings. Bring to the boil, then simmer gently, skimming frequently. Continue simmering until the liquid is reduced by half then pass through a fine sieve or muslin. Season to taste with salt and black pepper.

❧ *Pithivier of Vegetables* ❧

Serves 4

50 ml (2 fl oz) double cream
1 tablespoon olive oil
15 g (½ oz) unsalted butter
100 g (4 oz) onions, finely
    chopped
2 cloves garlic, crushed
100 g (4 oz) leek, diced
salt and freshly ground black
    pepper
100 g (4 oz) courgettes, diced

100 g (4 oz) mushrooms,
    chopped
225 g (8 oz) plum tomatoes,
    peeled, de-seeded and diced
2 tablespoons tomato purée
3–4 tablespoons chopped
    coriander leaves
500 g (1 lb 2 oz) puff pastry
1 egg yolk, beaten with
        1 teaspoon water and a pinch
        of salt

TO SERVE
Dressing (opposite)
balsamic vinegar
sprigs of chervil, to garnish

Place the cream in a small saucepan and boil to reduce by half. Leave to cool. Heat the oil and butter in a saucepan and sweat the onion in it for 7–8 minutes, then add the garlic and cook for a further 1 minute. Add the leeks, season generously with salt and black pepper and sweat for a further 2 minutes. Add the courgettes, mushrooms, diced tomatoes, tomato purée and coriander leaves. Cook for a further 10–15 minutes until the vegetables are tender and there is no liquid in the saucepan. Leave to go cool, then stir in the cream and adjust seasoning if necessary. Leave until cold.

Pre-heat the oven to gas mark 8, 450°F (230°C).

On a lightly floured surface, roll out the pastry to a thickness of 3 mm (⅛ in) and cut out 8 × 15 cm (6 in) rounds. Spoon the filling into the centre of 4 rounds, piling it high. Brush the edges of the pastry with beaten egg yolk and set the remaining pastry rounds on top of the filling. Press the edges well to seal, then cut a small air-hole in the top of each vegetable parcel. Make a decorative scalloped edge using a knife or cutter. Using a small, sharp knife, cut small slashes radiating from the centre of each parcel to the edge.

Set the pithiviers on a buttered baking tray and brush with beaten egg yolk. Chill in the refrigerator for about 20 minutes, then brush with the remaining egg yolk. Bake the pithiviers in the oven for about 20 minutes, until risen and golden-brown.

To serve, set a pithivier in the centre of each warmed plate. Spoon some Dressing around each one and drizzle the dressing with a little balsamic vinegar. Garnish with sprigs of chervil and serve at once.

Dressing

50 ml (2 fl oz) extra virgin olive
  oil
25 ml (1 fl oz) sherry vinegar
100 g (4 oz) plum tomatoes,
  peeled, de-seeded and diced

1 tablespoon chopped parsley
1 tablespoon chopped chervil
1 tablespoon chopped chives
salt and freshly ground black
  pepper

Whisk the olive oil and sherry vinegar together. Stir in the diced tomatoes and herbs and season to taste with salt and black pepper. Warm gently.

❧ *Fig Tart* ❧
Raspberry Coulis

Serves 6

SWEET PASTRY
100 g (4 oz) unsalted butter, cut
  into small dice
150 g (5 oz) plain flour, sifted
50 g (2 oz) caster sugar
1 egg yolk

TO SERVE
icing sugar for dusting
Raspberry Coulis (see p. 68)
6 'quenelles' of vanilla ice cream
  (or cinnamon ice cream)

FILLING
6 fresh figs, washed and dried
2 eggs
75 g (3 oz) caster sugar
120 ml (4 fl oz) milk
150 g (5 oz) crème fraiche

shreds of cinnamon stick
yoghurt and 6 sprigs of mint, to
  decorate

For the pastry, on a cold surface mix the butter to a dough with the flour, caster sugar and egg yolk. Cover with cling film and chill in the refrigerator for 30 minutes. On a lightly floured surface, roll out to a thickness of 3 mm (⅛ in) and use to line a 20 cm (8 in) flan tin. Chill again for at least 20 minutes.

Pre-heat the oven to gas mark 7, 425°F (220°C).

Cover the pastry with foil or greaseproof paper cut to fit and weighed down with dried beans. Bake blind for about 10 minutes, then remove the beans and bake for a further 5 minutes. Leave to cool. Cut the figs into 6 mm (¼ in) slices, discarding the end pieces, and arrange in concentric circles in the flan case.

Reduce the oven temperature to gas mark 5, 375°F (190°C).

Beat together the eggs, caster sugar, milk and crème fraiche until smooth. Pour the mixture carefully over the figs and bake for about 40 minutes until lightly golden and just set.

To serve, dust the edges of the pastry with icing sugar and cut the tart into 6 portions. Set a piece of tart on each plate, then spoon a little Raspberry Coulis beside it and place 3 tiny dots of yoghurt on the coulis. Run a skewer through the dots to give a decorative effect. Set a quenelle of vanilla or cinnamon ice cream beside each portion and top with some shreds of cinnamon stick. Decorate with a sprig of mint.

Raspberry Coulis
275 g (10 oz) raspberries
2 teaspoons lemon juice
40 g (1½ oz) icing sugar

Purée the raspberries in a liquidiser, then add the lemon juice and icing sugar. Pass through a fine sieve or muslin.

❧ *Canapés and Frivolities* ❧

Puff Pastry Hearts and Discs

Makes about 40 shapes

150 g (5 oz) puff pastry
1 egg yolk, beaten
2 teaspoons poppy seeds
2 teaspoons sesame seeds
1 teaspoon paprika

FILLING (OPTIONAL)
Stilton mixed with an equal
    quantity of butter, cream
    cheese or pâte

On a lightly floured surface, roll out the pastry to a thickness of about 3 mm (⅛ in). Brush with the beaten egg and divide into 3 pieces. Sprinkle one piece with the poppy seeds, one with the sesame seeds and the other with the paprika. Leave to rest in a cool place for 10–15 minutes. Stamp out hearts and discs using small pastry cutters. Arrange on buttered baking trays and leave to rest for 2 hours.

Pre-heat the oven to gas mark 7, 425°F (220°C).

Bake the pastry shapes for about 10 minutes, until crisp and golden. If wished, split and fill them with a mixture of equal quantities of Stilton and softened butter, beaten to a smooth 'pâte', or with cream cheese or softened pâte.

Prawns with Sage Leaves

Makes 20

10 rashers streaky bacon
40 sage leaves
20 uncooked prawns (or
    langoustines), peeled and
    deveined

20 button mushrooms
oil for deep-frying

TO SERVE
Rouille (see p. 55)

Remove the rinds from the bacon rashers and, with the back of a knife, stretch each rasher. Cut each rasher in half crossways. Place 2 sage leaves on each prawn, then wrap a piece of bacon around each one. Thread a mushroom and then a prawn on to each of 20 skewers. Deep-fry the skewers until the bacon is golden and the prawns are pink. Alternatively, brush with oil and cook under a grill pre-heated to high. Drain on absorbent paper.

Serve with Rouille handed separately.

Chicken Skewers with Bacon

Makes 40

200 g (7 oz) skinless, boneless
    chicken breast
200 g (7 oz) chicken livers
salt and freshly ground black
    pepper
10 rashers streaky bacon

½ quantity Chicken Rounds
    (see p. 70)
40 quail's eggs
40 bay leaves
40 sage leaves
melted butter to glaze

TO SERVE
Japanese pickled ginger

Cut the chicken into 40 small cubes. Cut the chicken livers into 40 pieces. Season both with salt and black pepper. Remove the rinds from the bacon rashers and cut each rasher in half lengthways and crossways. Wrap a piece of bacon around each piece of chicken liver.

Using floured hands, roll the chicken rounds mixture into 40 small balls. Cook the quail's eggs in boiling, salted water for 3 minutes. Drain and refresh in iced water, then drain and peel. Thread each of 40 bamboo skewers with a chicken round, a piece of bacon-wrapped liver, a bay leaf, a quail's egg, a sage leaf and a piece of chicken.

Brush lightly with melted butter and cook under a grill pre-heated to high, for about 5 minutes.

CHICKEN ROUNDS

Makes about 400 g (14 oz)
1 tablespoon oil
50 g (2 oz) onion, finely chopped
1 clove garlic, chopped
6 coriander stalks, chopped
6 parsley stalks, chopped

300 g (11 oz) boneless chicken
    meat from the legs, chopped
1 egg yolk
3 tablespoons double cream
salt and freshly ground black
    pepper

Heat the oil in a small saucepan and sweat the onion in it until translucent. Add the garlic and sweat for a further minute. Add the coriander and parsley stalks. Leave to cool, then mix with the chicken.

Mince the mixture through a medium mincer plate or whiz in a food processor. Place the mixture in a bowl set over a bowl of ice and beat in the egg yolk, then the cream. Season generously with salt and black pepper.

Paillettes

Makes about 50

250 g (9 oz) puff pastry
1 egg, beaten
50 g (2 oz) Parmesan cheese,
    finely grated

1½ teaspoons chopped
    rosemary
1½ teaspoons chopped sage
1 teaspoon paprika
2 teaspoons caraway seeds

On a lightly floured surface, roll out the pastry to a thickness of about 3 mm (⅛ in). Cut into 3 portions and brush each portion with beaten egg. Sprinkle all 3 portions with Parmesan cheese, then sprinkle one with a mixture of rosemary and sage, and one with a mixture of paprika and caraway seeds. Leave one portion with just Parmesan cheese.

Pre-heat the oven to gas mark 6, 400°F (200°C).

Fold each portion of pastry in half, then roll out again to a thickness of 3 mm (⅛ in). Cut each piece into strips about 15 cm (6 in) long and 6 mm (¼ in) wide, then twist each strip. Chill for 20 minutes in the refrigerator. Place the pastry twists on lightly greased baking sheets and bake for 10–12 minutes until golden-brown.

Raspberry and Mango Tartlets

Makes about 30

100 g (4 oz) Sweet Pastry
(see p. 67)
2½ tablespoons mascarpone
cheese (or crème fraiche)
75 raspberries

tiny sprigs of mint
icing sugar for dusting
1 small mango, peeled and thinly
sliced
1 strawberry

Pre-heat the oven to gas mark 5, 375°F (190°C).

On a lightly floured surface, roll out the pastry to a thickness of 3 mm (⅛ in) and use to line 15 × 4 cm (1½ in) square tartlet tins and 15 diamond-shaped ones. Trim the edges to neaten them and prick the base of each pastry case with a fork. Chill in the refrigerator for at least 20 minutes. Place the tartlet tins on a baking tray and bake in the oven for about 20 minutes until golden-brown. Leave to cool, then remove from the tins.

Spoon a tiny amount of mascarpone cheese into each tartlet. Place 5 raspberries in the square cases and decorate each with a sprig of mint dusted with icing sugar. Top the diamond-shaped cases with wafer-thin slices of mango, cut to shape, and decorate with tiny pieces of strawberry and mint leaf.

Cape Gooseberries in Caramel

Makes 20

20 Cape gooseberries
225 g (8 oz) caster sugar
a generous pinch of cream of
tartar

Peel back the lantern-shaped cover from each fruit and twist it.

Place the caster sugar in a saucepan and add the cream of tartar and 2 tablespoons water. Heat gently until the sugar dissolves, then boil until the syrup is a medium caramel colour. Immediately place the saucepan in a bowl of cold water to prevent the syrup getting any darker. Quickly dip each Cape gooseberry in the caramel.

Leave on a lightly buttered tray to set hard.

Paul Gayler

Now at the new Lanesborough Hotel in London, with its two restaurants *The Dining Room* and *The Conservatory*, Paul Gayler started his culinary career at the tender age of twelve. His father, a free-lance toast-master, and his mother set up a once-a-week catering business, and Paul helped to prepare basic roasts. He was soon certain where his future would lie. After a basic training, he worked under first Remy Fougère at the Royal Garden Hotel, then Anton Mosimann at The Dorchester. From the former, he absorbed the foundations of classical cuisine; from the latter, the new style of lightness and the art of presentation.

During his many successful years at Inigo Jones in Covent Garden he explored traditional British dishes – an exploration that has culminated in the desserts, inspired by Mrs Beeton, that are served in The Dining Room. It is also responsible for his development of a gourmet vegetarian menu. Paul was one of the first major chefs to give proper consideration to this area and there is now a multitude of vegetarian dishes on the menu of The Conservatory. Increasingly, he is acknowledged to be one of the leading exponents of good vegetable cooking. Although not vegetarian himself, he has drawn together flavourings, ideas and characteristics from many cuisines – among them Italian, Hungarian, French and oriental – to demonstrate how eclectic and uniquely satisfying imaginative vegetarian cooking can be.

Paul Gayler with, from left: Oriental Black Risotto with Vegetable Garnish (page 76), Salade of Roasted Vegetables (page 79) and Ricotta and Spinach Gnocchi with Walnut and Sage Pesto (page 74).

🌺 *Ricotta and Spinach Gnocchi* 🌺
Walnut and Sage Pesto

Serves 4

100 g (4 oz) unsalted butter	freshly ground black pepper
135 g (4 ¾ oz) plain flour	3 eggs
salt	1 egg yolk
3 tablespoons ricotta cheese	4 tablespoons double cream
½ garlic clove, crushed	2 tablespoons grated Parmesan
225 g (8 oz) spinach, cooked,	cheese
squeezed dry and chopped	

TO SERVE

Walnut and Sage Pesto (below)	1 red and 1 yellow tomato,
12 deep-fried sage leaves, to	skinned, de-seeded and cut
garnish	into diamonds, to garnish

For the gnocchi, place 90 g (3½ oz) of the butter and 175 ml (6 fl oz) water in a saucepan. Bring to the boil, then sprinkle the flour over and add a pinch of salt. Mix to a smooth paste over the heat, then add the ricotta. Leave to cool. Heat the remaining butter in another pan and add the garlic and spinach. Stir well and season with salt and black pepper. Leave to cool. Mix the 3 eggs into the ricotta mixture one at a time, then add the spinach. Leave to go cold. Shape oval dumplings of gnocchi with a hot, wet teaspoon, or pipe 2.5 cm (1 in) lengths with a piping-bag fitted with a large plain nozzle. Drop the dumplings into boiling, salted water, then poach for 10 minutes. Drain thoroughly. Arrange the gnocchi in an ovenproof dish or on individual heatproof serving plates. Beat the egg yolk, cream and Parmesan cheese together and use to coat the gnocchi. Pre-heat the grill to high and grill the gnocchi until golden.

To serve, drizzle with Walnut and Sage Pesto and garnish with the deep-fried sage leaves and tomato diamonds.

Walnut and Sage Pesto

50 g (2 oz) shelled walnuts	1 teaspoon lemon juice
2 tablespoons sage leaves	salt and freshly ground black
2 cloves garlic, crushed	pepper
200 ml (7 fl oz) olive oil	

Blend the walnuts, sage leaves and garlic in a food processor. Gradually add the oil and blend to a thick soup consistency. Add the lemon juice and season to taste with salt and black pepper.

Cannelloni of Ratatouille, Creamed Goat's Cheese and Basil

Serves 4

4 tablespoons olive oil
65 g (2½ oz) unsalted butter, cut into small pieces
1 small onion, finely diced
1 clove garlic, crushed
1 courgette, cut into 6 mm (¼ in) dice
½ small aubergine, cut into 6 mm (¼ in) dice
½ red pepper, cut into 6 mm (¼ in) dice
½ green pepper, cut into 6 mm (¼ in) dice
2 tablespoons double cream

12 finely shredded basil leaves
4 unshredded basil leaves
50 g (2 oz) fresh goat's cheese (passed through a sieve or mashed with a fork)
8 sheets fresh lasagne (see p. 76) (or dried lasagne), cooked
salt and freshly ground black pepper
4 tablespoons vegetable stock (or water)
freshly shaved Parmesan cheese, to garnish

Pre-heat the oven to gas mark 6, 400°F (200°C).

Heat half of the olive oil with 15 g (½ oz) of the butter in a heavy-based saucepan, then add the onion and garlic and cook gently together for 1 minute. Add the diced courgette, aubergine and peppers. Cook rapidly until all the vegetables are tender. Remove from the saucepan and leave to cool.

Place the cream in another saucepan with 8 of the finely shredded basil leaves and boil to reduce by half. Add the goat's cheese and mix well, then mix in the cooled ratatouille. Leave to one side to go cold.

Lay the cooked sheets of lasagne on a clean tea-towel and pat dry. Brush with olive oil and season with salt and black pepper. Spread each sheet with some of the goat's cheese and ratatouille mixture and roll each one up. Place these cannelloni in a well-buttered ovenproof dish with the 4 unshredded basil leaves, the vegetable stock or water and the remaining olive oil. Cover with buttered foil then place in the oven for about 10 minutes until warmed.

To serve, remove the cannelloni from the oven and arrange 2 on each of 4 plates. Pour the juices from the cannelloni into a small saucepan and heat gently. Whisk in the remaining butter, a little at a time, to give a creamy sauce – the butter must not melt. Season to taste, then pass through a fine strainer. Add the remaining finely shredded basil leaves and pour over the cannelloni. Garnish with the Parmesan cheese and serve immediately.

FRESH LASAGNE

250 g (9 oz) strong plain flour
2 eggs
1 egg yolk

1 tablespoon oil
1 teaspoon water
a pinch of salt

Place the flour in a bowl, make a well in the centre and break in the eggs and egg yolk, then add the oil, water and salt. Mix the flour in gradually towards the centre to amalgamate all the ingredients to a paste. Cover and leave to rest for up to 1 hour before use.

Roll out the dough through a pasta machine (or, more tediously, by hand) into the required shape ready for use.

❊ *Oriental Black Risotto* ❊
Vegetable Garnish

Serves 4

40 g (1½ oz) unsalted butter
1 small onion, finely chopped
½ teaspoon finely chopped
    garlic
½ teaspoon finely chopped root
    ginger
225 g (8 oz) Basmati rice

2 teaspoons Chinese five-spice
    powder
750 ml (1¼ pints) Brown
    Mushroom Stock (opposite)
salt and freshly ground black
    pepper

TO SERVE
2 – 3 tablespoons dark soy sauce
Vegetable Garnish (opposite)
16 coriander leaves

Heat the butter in a large, heavy-based saucepan, then add the onion, garlic and ginger. Cook together for 1 minute without browning. Add the rice and stir well, then add the five-spice powder and mix well. Pour in the brown mushroom stock and bring to the boil, stirring occasionally. Add a little salt and black pepper, reduce the heat and allow the rice to simmer until it is cooked and nearly all of the stock has evaporated. Stir frequently with a wooden spoon.

To serve, add soy sauce to taste to the rice, then arrange on plates or in bowls. Add the Vegetable Garnish, reserved mushrooms from the Vegetable Garnish and coriander leaves and serve at once.

BROWN MUSHROOM STOCK

75 g (3 oz) unsalted butter
4 shallots, shredded
1 large clove garlic, sliced
350 g (12 oz) button
    mushrooms, finely chopped
1.25 kg (2½ lb) flat mushrooms,
    finely chopped

1 tablespoon tomato purée
3 ripe tomatoes, chopped
18 coriander stalks
salt and freshly ground black
    pepper

Heat the butter in a saucepan, then add the shallots and garlic and sweat without colouring. Add all the mushrooms and cook, stirring well, until the mushrooms are deep brown and slightly caramelised. This will take about 15 minutes. Add the tomato purée and tomatoes and mix well. Cover and continue cooking gently for about 10 minutes.

Pour in 1.5 litres (2½ pints) cold water and add the coriander stalks. Bring to the boil. Skim well to remove any impurities that rise to the surface, then reduce the heat and simmer for a further 15–20 minutes. Strain the stock through a very fine sieve.

Vegetable Garnish

4 tablespoons sesame oil
40 g (1½ oz) unsalted butter
14 small shiitake mushrooms,
    halved
½ teaspoon finely chopped
    garlic
½ teaspoon finely chopped root
    ginger
25 g (1 oz) bean sprouts

1 small carrot, finely shredded
12 mange tout, finely shredded
¼ red pepper, finely shredded
¼ green pepper, finely shredded
10 g (¼ oz) daikon radish
    (mooli), finely shredded
2 spring onions, finely shredded
salt and freshly ground black
    pepper

Heat a frying-pan and add 1 tablespoon of the sesame oil and 15 g (½ oz) of the butter. Sauté the mushrooms, then put them to one side and keep warm. They will be served separately. Heat the remaining oil and butter in the same frying-pan, then add the garlic and ginger. Take off the heat and allow to infuse for a few minutes, then add the bean sprouts and vegetables. Sauté until cooked but crisp. Season with salt and black pepper.

❧ Crisp Napoleon of ❧ Vegetables
Goulash Sauce

Serves 4

150 g (5 oz) puff pastry	16 mange tout, trimmed
1 medium-size green courgette	12 asparagus tips, trimmed
1 medium-size yellow courgette	25 g (1 oz) broad beans, skinned
(or a little vegetable squash)	50 g (2 oz) unsalted butter,
1 large carrot	melted
1 large turnip	paprika
8 tiny broccoli florets	salt and freshly ground black
8 tiny cauliflower florets	pepper
8 baby sweetcorn, halved	

TO SERVE
Goulash Sauce (below)

Pre-heat the oven to gas mark 4, 350°F (180°C).

Roll the pastry to a 25 cm × 13 cm (10 in × 5 in) rectangle about 3 mm (⅛ in) thick, then cut the rectangle into quarters to make 4 × 13 cm × 6 cm (5 in × 2½ in) shapes. Bake on a buttered baking sheet for 5 minutes. Cool for a maximum of 5 minutes, then ease each pastry strip into 3–5 layers. Cut the courgettes, carrot and turnip into 1 cm × 4 cm (½ in × 1½ in) cylinder shapes. Blanch all the vegetables separately in boiling, salted water and refresh in iced water. Drain and dry well.

Reset the oven to gas mark 5, 375°F (190°C). Brush the pastry rectangles generously with melted butter and dust lightly with paprika. Bake for 8–10 minutes until crispy. Sauté the vegetables quickly in the remaining butter to warm them.

To serve, layer 3 sheets of each pastry rectangle with a quarter of the vegetables and arrange on a plate. Pour some Goulash Sauce around each portion and serve at once.

Goulash Sauce

1 shallot, sliced	1 teaspoon paprika
½ clove garlic, crushed	¼ teaspoon caraway seeds
½ large red pepper, de-seeded	120 ml (4 fl oz) dry white wine
and chopped	1 teaspoon tomato purée
1 large ripe tomato, quartered	200 ml (7 fl oz) White Vegetable
and de-seeded	Stock (opposite)
20 g (¾ oz) unsalted butter	120 ml (4 fl oz) double cream.

Sweat the shallot, garlic, pepper and tomato in the butter. Stir in the paprika, caraway seeds and wine and boil rapidly to reduce by half. Add the tomato purée and simmer for 3–4 minutes. Stir in the vegetable stock. Bring to the boil and skim off any impurities on the surface. Reduce the heat and simmer gently for 10–15 minutes. Blend in a food processor until smooth, then pass through a fine sieve. Just before serving, bring the sauce back to the boil, half-whip the cream and whisk it into the sauce until frothy.

WHITE VEGETABLE STOCK
Makes 1 litre (1¾ pints)

2 tablespoons olive oil	1 clove garlic, finely diced
1 onion, finely diced	4 black peppercorns
1 small leek, finely diced	1 small bay leaf
2 celery stalks, finely diced	1 sprig of thyme
2 carrots, finely diced	1 teaspoon sea salt
75 g (3 oz) white cabbage, finely diced	

Place the olive oil in a large saucepan and add the vegetables. Cook gently for about 5 minutes until soft. Add the diced garlic, peppercorns, bay leaf and thyme, then add 1.5 litres (2½ pints) cold water. Bring to the boil, add the salt and cook for 30–45 minutes or until the liquid is reduced by one-third. Pour the stock through a fine strainer and cool. Chill until required.

Salade of Roasted Vegetables
Mozzarella, Tapenade, Polenta Croûtons

Serves 4

1 clove garlic, halved	1 green courgette, cut into 6 mm (¼ in) slices
2 tablespoons olive oil	½ red pepper, de-seeded and cut into diamonds
16 asparagus tips, trimmed	75 g (3 oz) wild mushrooms
1 small aubergine, cut into batons – use only the outside	8–12 cherry tomatoes
1 yellow courgette, cut into 6 mm (¼ in) slices	salt and freshly ground black pepper

TO SERVE
rocket leaves
4 slices French bread
4 slices mozzarella cheese
Tomato Vinaigrette (see p. 80)

Tapenade (see p. 80)
Polenta Croûtons (see p. 80), to garnish

Pre-heat the oven to gas mark 6, 400°F (200°C). Rub a heavy-based ovenproof pan with the garlic. Heat the olive oil in it, then toss the vegetables in the oil to colour them lightly. Season with salt and black pepper and cook in the oven for 4–5 minutes until golden. Remove and keep warm.

To serve, dress some rocket leaves with a little Tomato Vinaigrette and place in the centre of each plate. Toast the French bread and top with the mozzarella. Melt slightly under a hot grill. Place about 1 tablespoon Tapenade on each croûton, and place each croûton on the rocket leaves. Arrange the roasted vegetables around the rocket salad, sprinkle with Tomato Vinaigrette and garnish with Polenta Croûtons.

Tomato Vinaigrette

2 large, very ripe tomatoes
½ clove garlic
1½ tablespoons balsamic
　　vinegar
½ teaspoon sugar
6 basil leaves

100 ml (3½ fl oz) olive oil
salt and freshly ground black
　　pepper
1 tablespoon tomato juice
　　(optional)

Cut the tomatoes into small pieces and place in a bowl with the garlic, vinegar, sugar and basil leaves. Leave to marinate for 1 hour in a warm place. Strain through a fine strainer into a clean bowl, then whisk in the olive oil. Season to taste with salt and black pepper and add tomato juice, if wished.

Tapenade

20 black olives, stoned
1 teaspoon capers
1 clove garlic

4 tablespoons olive oil
1 tablespoon chopped parsley
freshly ground black pepper

Roughly chop the olives and capers and blend with the garlic in a food processor, then add the olive oil and chopped parsley. Season with pepper.

Polenta Croûtons

250 ml (8 fl oz) milk
1 clove garlic
salt

a pinch of nutmeg
75 g (3 oz) polenta
40 g (1½ oz) unsalted butter

Bring the milk to the boil with the garlic, salt and nutmeg. Rain in the polenta and mix until smooth, then reduce the heat and cook in a double boiler for 8–10 minutes. Spread the polenta in a well-buttered dish until it is about 1 cm (½ in) thick. Allow it to go cold, then cut into 1 cm (½ in) croûtons. Just before serving, fry in the butter until golden-brown.

*Paul Gayler's Tea Blancmange with Grapefruit Syrup
and Candied Rind (page 86).*

❧ *Baked Apple Dumplings* ❧
Apricot Purée, Butterscotch Sauce

Serves 4

6 dried apricots, washed and cut
    into 6 mm (¼ in) dice
2 tablespoons flaked almonds,
    lightly toasted
2 tablespoons dark rum
1 tablespoon caster sugar
1 tablespoon sultanas
4 Granny Smith apples

225 g (8 oz) sugar
a squeeze of lemon juice
6 sheets filo pastry approx.
    50 cm × 25 cm
    (20 in × 10 in)
50 g (2 oz) unsalted butter,
    melted
ground mixed spice

TO SERVE
Apricot Purée (opposite)
Butterscotch Sauce (opposite)
1 tablespoon flaked almonds,
    lightly toasted

Pre-heat the oven to gas mark 6, 400°F (200°C).

Place the diced apricots in a bowl with the flaked almonds, dark rum, caster sugar and sultanas. Mix well and leave to soak for about an hour.

Peel the apples carefully, taking care not to lose their shape, then remove the stalks but do not throw them away. Remove the central core and poach the apples in 600 ml (1 pint) water with the sugar and a squeeze of lemon juice for about 5 minutes. They should still be firm to the touch. Remove the apples from the poaching syrup and allow them to cool. Reserve the syrup. When the apples are cold, fill the cavity of each one with the marinated fruit mixture.

Lay out 1 sheet of the filo pastry on a work surface, brush it generously with melted butter, then top it with another sheet of pastry. Add a third sheet of pastry and brush with melted butter. Cut the layered sheet into 2 small squares. Make 2 more squares with the remaining 3 sheets of pastry.

Place 1 apple in the centre of each pastry square and fold it up to enclose the apple. Brush lightly with melted butter and delicately sprinkle with mixed spice. Place on a baking sheet and bake for about 20 minutes until the apples are tender and the pastry is lightly golden.

To serve, place an apple on each of 4 plates. Pour a little Apricot Purée around each one, then spoon dots of Butterscotch Sauce on top of the purée. Using a skewer, draw a line through each dot to give a decorative effect. Decorate with the remaining flaked almonds, and replace the apple stalks before serving.

Apricot Purée

4 fresh apricots, halved and
stoned

5 tablespoons poaching syrup
from the apples

Poach the apricots in the poaching syrup until soft. Blend in a food processor until smooth, then pass through a fine sieve.

Butterscotch Sauce

40 g (1½ oz) brown sugar
3 tablespoons double cream

40 g (1½ oz) unsalted butter
¼ teaspoon vanilla essence

Place all the ingredients in a heavy-based pan and cook, stirring, for 3–5 minutes until the colour changes to light caramel.

🌺 *Orange Soufflés* 🌺
Orange Sabayon, Marmalade Sauce

Serves 8

200 ml (7 fl oz) milk
150 g (5 oz) caster sugar plus
extra for the dariole moulds
½ vanilla pod, split
finely grated rind and juice of
1 orange

65 g (2½ oz) unsalted butter
65 g (2½ oz) plain flour
juice of ½ lemon
4 eggs, separated
butter for greasing

TO SERVE
Orange Sabayon (see p. 84)
Marmalade Sauce (see p. 84)
4 sprigs of mint

Pre-heat the oven to gas mark 4, 350°F (180°C).

Bring the milk, half of the caster sugar, the vanilla pod and the orange rind to the boil, then leave to cool and allow the flavours to infuse. In another saucepan, melt the butter and stir in the flour to make a roux. Cook over gentle heat, stirring, for 1 minute. Take off the heat. Remove the vanilla pod from the milk and pour the milk on to the roux. Mix well until smooth. Add the orange and lemon juices and return the sauce to the heat. Bring to the boil and cook, stirring all the time, for 2–3 minutes until the sauce thickens. Allow it to cool slightly, then beat in the egg yolks. Whisk the egg whites until stiff, then whisk in the remaining caster sugar, a little at a time, until thick and glossy. Beat half the egg whites into the sauce, then carefully fold in the remaining half until evenly combined.

Lightly butter and sugar 8 individual dariole moulds, then fill them two-thirds full with the soufflé mixture. Place in a roasting tin and pour in hot water to come at least halfway up the moulds. Cook in the oven for 20 minutes until risen and lightly set.

To serve, unmould each soufflé on to a plate. Coat each one with a little of the Orange Sabayon and spoon a little Marmalade Sauce on to each plate. Decorate each soufflé with a sprig of mint.

Orange Sabayon

2 egg yolks
finely grated rind and juice of
    1 orange

25 g (1 oz) caster sugar
orange liqueur (optional)

Whisk all the ingredients, except the orange liqueur if using, with 2 tablespoons hot water in a bowl over warm water until they increase to 3–4 times their original volume. Continue whisking until the mixture thickens but do not let it boil. Stir in orange liqueur to taste, if wished.

Marmalade Sauce

4 tablespoons orange
    marmalade

Heat the marmalade with 2–3 tablespoons water to a sauce consistency. Keep warm.

❧ *Dried Fruit and Ginger Pudding* ❧
Vanilla Custard Sauce

Serves 6–8

90 g (3½ oz) dried stoned dates,
    diced
90 g (3½ oz) dried figs, diced
40 g (1½ oz) stem ginger, diced
2 tablespoons raisins
½ teaspoon bicarbonate of soda
1 teaspoon baking powder
½ teaspoon vanilla essence

65 g (2½ oz) unsalted butter,
    softened
65 g (2½ oz) caster sugar
2 eggs, beaten
175 g (6 oz) self-raising flour,
    sifted
icing sugar for dusting

TO SERVE
Vanilla Custard Sauce (opposite)

Pre-heat the oven to gas mark 5, 375°F (190°C).

Mix together the dates, figs and ginger, then stir in 250 ml (8 fl oz) boiling water. Add the raisins, then the bicarbonate of soda, baking powder and vanilla essence. Leave to stand.

Cream the butter and caster sugar until pale, then beat in the eggs and fold in the flour. Stir the fruit mixture with all its liquid into the egg mixture and transfer to a well-buttered 18 cm (7 in) diameter cake tin or china dish. Stand the tin in a roasting tin and pour hot water in to come at least halfway up the tin. Bake for about 45 minutes until risen and firm to the touch.

To serve, unmould the pudding on to a plate and dust with icing sugar. Serve with the Vanilla Custard Sauce.

Vanilla Custard Sauce

450 ml (15 fl oz) mixed milk and
    double cream
1 vanilla pod, split

4 egg yolks
50–100 g (2–4 oz) caster sugar

Bring the milk and cream and the vanilla pod to the boil, remove from the heat and leave to infuse for a few minutes. Remove the vanilla pod. Beat the egg yolks with sugar to taste, then stir the warm milk and cream into the egg mixture. Return to the heat and cook, stirring, until thick enough to coat the back of a wooden spoon. Do not let the sauce boil.

❧ Fruit Puddings ❧
Blackberry Sauce

Serves 6

12 thin slices white bread, crusts
    removed
100 g (4 oz) sugar
juice of 1 lemon
75 g (3 oz) blackberries
75 g (3 oz) raspberries
175 g (6 oz) apples, peeled, cored
    and cut into small slices

75 g (3 oz) pear, peeled, cored
    and cut into small slices
75 g (3 oz) plums, stoned and
    cut into small slices
2 leaves gelatine, soaked in water
    to soften
50 ml (2 fl oz) English rosewater

TO SERVE
Blackberry Sauce (see p. 86)
whipped cream

6 sprigs of mint
fresh raspberries (optional)

Cut the bread into wide fingers and use to line 6 individual dariole moulds. Reserve the bread trimmings to cover the tops of the puddings.

Mix the sugar and lemon juice in a saucepan with 120 ml (4 fl oz) water and heat gently to dissolve the sugar. Bring to the boil to make a light syrup. Poach the blackberries and raspberries for 30 seconds. Remove them from the syrup and poach the apples, pear and plums for about 2 minutes until just tender. Combine all the fruit and use to fill the bread-lined moulds.

Reduce the syrup by boiling it for 1–2 minutes until slightly thickened. Remove from the heat and add the soaked gelatine and rosewater. Stir until the gelatine is dissolved, then pour the liquid over the fruit so that it soaks into the bread. Cover the tops of the puddings with the reserved bread trimmings. Cover each pudding with cling film or greaseproof paper and press down with a small weight. Chill overnight in the refrigerator.

To serve, unmould each pudding on to a plate and spoon some Blackberry Sauce on top. Decorate with whipped cream and a sprig of mint. If wished, add extra raspberries to each plate.

Blackberry Sauce
100 g (4 oz) caster sugar
150 g (5 oz) blackberries
lemon juice to taste

Dissolve the sugar in 120 ml (4 fl oz) water over gentle heat, then boil for 1–2 minutes. Add the blackberries and cook until soft. Blend in a food processor and pass through a fine sieve. Add lemon juice to taste.

Tea Blancmange
Grapefruit Syrup and Candied Rind

Makes 8

BLANCMANGE
250 ml (8 fl oz) milk
65 g (2½ oz) caster sugar
1 tablespoon Darjeeling tea
    leaves
4 egg yolks

4 leaves gelatine, soaked in water
    to soften
juice of ¼ orange
juice of ½ lemon
250 ml (8 fl oz) double cream,
    lightly whipped

TEA JELLY
75 g (3 oz) caster sugar
2 teaspoons Darjeeling tea
    leaves

2 leaves gelatine, soaked in water
    to soften

TO SERVE
Grapefruit Syrup and Candied
   Rind (below)
yellow and pink grapefruit
   segments
whipped cream
8 sprigs of mint

For the blancmange, boil the milk with half of the caster sugar, then add the tea leaves. Remove from the heat and leave to infuse. Whisk the egg yolks and remaining caster sugar together until thick and pale, then stir the milk into the mixture. Return to the heat and cook, stirring, until the mixture coats the back of a wooden spoon. Do not let it boil. Remove from the heat and add the gelatine. Stir until the gelatine dissolves. Strain through a very fine sieve to remove the tea, and leave to cool. When the mixture is cool, stir in the orange and lemon juices and, when it is nearly set, fold in the lightly whipped cream. Set 8 deep 6 cm (2½ in) rings on a tray and spoon in the mixture. Level the surfaces and chill in the refrigerator.

For the tea jelly, combine the caster sugar and 6 tablespoons water and bring to the boil to give a light syrup. Add the tea leaves, take off the heat, and leave to infuse. Add the gelatine and stir until dissolved. Pass through a fine sieve and as soon as it is cool, but not yet starting to set, spoon a little on to each mousse. Chill in the refrigerator until lightly set.

Alternatively, use individual dariole moulds instead of rings. Spoon a little tea jelly into each one and allow it to set before adding the blancmange.

To serve, unmould the puddings on to individual plates. Spoon a little Grapefruit Syrup around each one, and decorate with Candied Rind, grapefruit segments, whipped cream and sprigs of mint.

Grapefruit Syrup and Candied Rind
6 grapefruit – preferably pink
225 g (8 oz) caster sugar

Pare the rind from 1 grapefruit and cut into fine julienne strips. Blanch in boiling water. Dissolve the sugar in the juice of all 6 grapefruit and boil to reduce to a light syrup. Cook the grapefruit julienne strips in a little of the syrup until tender and translucent. Leave to cool.

Rosamund Grant

ROSAMUND GRANT FIRST LEARNED to appreciate the unique flavours and aromas of Caribbean cooking as a child in Guyana, but it was not until her early twenties, whilst living in France, that cooking became a serious interest for her.

The style that characterises Rosamund's cuisine draws on these influences and also those gained whilst travelling abroad, tasting, cooking and collecting recipes from countries such as Ghana, North America and Jamaica, and also from friends and relatives sharing with her their own knowledge of cooking styles and methods.

Her cuisine has its genesis in Africa, but has followed the paths of the African peoples to the Caribbean islands, to South and North America and to Europe.

Rosamund has been a pioneer in acknowledging and exploring these indisputable links of black culinary history. Her restaurant in North London, *Bambaya*, offers a selection of dishes which enables the diner to embark on a journey of taste from one continent to another.

Some of Rosamund's recipes are traditional, faithfully reproducing an island or soul-food dish. Many more of her recipes are originals, created in her own inimitable style but still using the traditions of fresh produce, well-marinated and seasoned meat and fish, and spicy sauces, their chilli heat tempered by coconut milk.

Rosamund Grant with, from left: Bambaya Groundnut Soup garnished with sliced, fresh chillies (page 90), Joloff Rice and Sauce, with vegetables (page 96) and Caribbean Baked Chicken (page 95).

🎇 Bambaya Groundnut Soup 🎇

Serves 4

6 tablespoons wholegrain
    groundnut paste (or
    wholegrain peanut butter)
1 teaspoon tomato purée
1 medium-size onion, chopped

1 teaspoon thyme leaves
2 small slices root ginger
2 bay leaves
salt and hot pepper to taste

Put the groundnut paste into a large saucepan and stir in 300 ml (10 fl oz) water. Heat until the water is just warm. Add the tomato purée and whisk until well mixed. Blend 300 ml (10 fl oz) water and the onion in a food processor and add to the saucepan. Add 1.4 litres (2½ pints) water and the thyme, ginger, bay leaves and hot pepper. Bring to the boil. Reduce the heat and cook, uncovered, for 30 minutes.

As the liquid reduces, some groundnut paste will be deposited on the sides of the saucepan. Stir well to incorporate it into the soup. Cook, uncovered, for a further 30 minutes, stirring occasionally, until reduced to 1.2 litres (2 pints). Season to taste with salt.

🎇 Coconut King Prawns 🎇

Serves 2–3

12 large uncooked prawns,
    peeled and deveined but
    with tails intact
2 cloves garlic, crushed
1 tablespoon lemon juice
salt and freshly ground black
    pepper to taste

4 tablespoons extra-fine
    desiccated coconut
2 tablespoons chopped chives
1 egg, beaten
oil for deep-frying

TO SERVE
lime or lemon slices or wedges,
    to garnish

Cut the prawns along the length of their backs without cutting right through them, to allow them to fan out. Rinse in cold water and pat dry. Marinate in the garlic, lemon juice, salt and black pepper for about 1 hour.

Mix together the coconut and chives. Dip each prawn into the beaten egg, then into the coconut and chive mixture. Fry the prawns in hot oil for about 1 minute only, until light golden-brown. Drain on kitchen paper.

To serve, garnish with lime or lemon slices.

🏵 *Spinach and Prawn* 🏵 *Creolese*

Serves 2

25 g (1 oz) butter
1 tablespoon oil
8 shallots, chopped
2 cloves garlic, crushed
2 plum tomatoes, peeled and
    chopped
½ teaspoon turmeric
1 long, red chilli, de-seeded and
    chopped
2 teaspoons shrimp paste
    (optional)
25 g (1 oz) dried shrimps, soaked
    in a little cold water for
    30 minutes

1 kg (2 lb) shell-on prawns,
    peeled, the heads reserved
    for the stock, seasoned with
    salt, freshly ground black
    pepper and the juice of
    ½ lime
4 tablespoons Stock (below) or
    water
2 tablespoons soy sauce
450 g (1 lb) young, tender
    spinach or callaloo, chopped

Put the butter and oil into a large frying-pan or wok. Add the shallots and garlic and cook gently for 8 minutes until they are a good golden-brown colour. Add the tomatoes, turmeric, chilli, shrimp paste if using, shrimps, prawns, stock and soy sauce. Cook for a further 5 minutes, stirring frequently, then add the spinach. Stir together and cook until the spinach is just wilted.

STOCK
heads from shell-on prawns
1 onion, roughly chopped
4 cloves
1 long, red chilli, de-seeded and
    chopped

Place all the ingredients in a large saucepan with 1.2 litres (2 pints) water. Bring to the boil, then reduce the heat and simmer, uncovered, for 15–20 minutes. Pass through a fine sieve.

Spinach and Pumpkin Creolese

Use 4 plum tomatoes (or medium-size tomatoes) instead of 2.
Use 225 g (8 oz) pumpkin, peeled and chopped, instead of shrimp paste, shrimps and prawns.
Add 300 ml (10 fl oz) vegetable stock.

Joloff Rice and Sauce

Serves 8

4 tablespoons vegetable oil
1 large onion, finely chopped
2 × 400 g (14 oz) tins chopped
   tomatoes (or 450 g/1 lb
   fresh plum tomatoes, peeled
   and chopped)
3 tablespoons tomato purée
½ large onion, roughly chopped

2 tablespoons dried shrimps,
   soaked in a little water for
   30 minutes, then drained
1½ teaspoons chopped thyme
900 ml (1½ pints) stock (or
   water)
a little grated nutmeg
450 g (1 lb) long-grain rice,
   washed
salt and hot pepper to taste

Heat the oil in a large saucepan, add the finely chopped onion and cook gently for 10 minutes until well softened. Add 1 tin of tomatoes (or the fresh ones, if using) and 2 tablespoons of the tomato purée. Stir well and simmer.

Meanwhile, in a food processor, liquidise the remaining tomatoes with the roughly chopped onion and the shrimps. Add to the saucepan and simmer for about 15 minutes, stirring occasionally. The sauce will reduce to a rich, thick consistency. Add the thyme, stock, nutmeg, salt and hot pepper. Bring to the boil, then cook for 30 minutes over a fairly moderate heat, allowing the sauce to reduce and thicken.

Place the rice in a separate saucepan. Scoop out about 450 ml (15 fl oz) of the sauce and add to the rice. Add the remaining tomato purée, 600 ml (1 pint) water, and salt to taste. Mix well and simmer, stirring occasionally with a fork, until most of the liquid is absorbed. Reduce the heat further, place a piece of foil on top of the rice and steam over a very low heat until the rice is cooked.

Rosamund Grant's Cucumber, Tomato and Avocado Salad
with Green Chilli and Lime Dressing (page 102).

Pre-heat the oven to gas mark 5, 375°F (190°C).

Sift the cornmeal, flour, baking powder, salt, demerara sugar and nutmeg together in a large bowl and mix well. Whisk the milk and egg together and pour into the flour mixture. Stir immediately with a wooden spoon. Add the melted butter and mix quickly until thoroughly incorporated.

Pour into a buttered 18 cm (7 in) diameter ovenproof dish (1.2 litre/2 pint capacity) and bake for 45 minutes until risen and golden-brown. It should be just firm to the touch.

Serve hot and buttered.

Cucumber, Tomato and Avocado Salad with Green Chilli and Lime Dressing

Serves 4–6

3 beef tomatoes, sliced
1 large, ripe avocado, peeled and sliced
1 cucumber, peeled and thinly sliced
1 medium-size red onion, thinly sliced
juice of ½ lemon (or ½ lime)
1 green chilli, de-seeded and finely chopped
½ teaspoon salt
freshly ground black pepper
chopped mint, to garnish

Arrange the sliced tomatoes and avocado on a plate. In a bowl, mix together the cucumber, onion, lemon juice, chilli, salt and black pepper. Arrange next to the tomatoes and avocado. Garnish with chopped mint.

Plantain Crisps

Serves 6—8

4 green plantains
oil for deep-frying
salt

Top and tail the plantains and cut them in half. Slit the skin of each half plantain lengthways in 3—4 places and peel away from the flesh. Cut the flesh into paper-thin slices with a slicer or sharp knife.

Heat the oil, preferably in a fryer with a basket. Carefully drop the rounds of plantain into the basket and fry until just golden-brown. Drain on kitchen paper, cool and sprinkle with salt.

Store in an airtight container until required.

Shaun Hill

B ORN IN ULSTER, but brought up in London, Shaun Hill came to cooking comparatively late, in his mid-teens. The motivating factors were greed, pleasure and money, not necessarily in that order. Turning down a place at university, he worked first at Carrier's in Islington, London, under a proprietor who, along with Elizabeth David, had been responsible for opening up new vistas to a whole generation of British chefs and home cooks. There Shaun discovered the wealth of good dishes in cuisines other than French, and also learned how to create flavours with herbs and spices.

After many years in a series of restaurants (including his own) whose names read like the index to a good restaurant guide, he came to rest at the inspired *Gidleigh Park* in Devon, a country house hotel on the edge of Dartmoor. There his eclectic culinary range and imagination have been allowed full rein. Despite its robust spicing and saucing, his cooking is produce- rather than dish-centred, an enthusiastic and loving celebration of the highest quality raw ingredients. His open ravioli topped with pan-fried chicken livers and deep-fried zest of lemon demonstrates that sophisticated flavours can emerge from less expensive ingredients. His signature dish of scallops with lentil and coriander sauce balances the fresh flavours of the scallops and herb with the earthiness of the lentils.

A Master Chef of Great Britain, Shaun Hill is one of the first British members of the *Académie Culinaire de France*.

Shaun Hill with, from left: Italian Bread (page 106),
Bourride of Chicken with Garlic Mayonnaise (page 114),
Caramel and Apple Tarts with Caramel Sauce and
Caramel Ice Cream (page 118) and Steamed Aylesbury
Duckling with Salad (page 112).

🏵 *Steamed Aylesbury Duckling* 🏵
Salad, Roast Salt and Pepper

Serves 2

1.75 kg (4 lb) Aylesbury
　　duckling, wishbone
　　removed
salt and freshly ground black
　　pepper
150 ml (5 fl oz) groundnut oil

50–75 g (2–3 oz) assorted salad
　　leaves such as lollo rosso or
　　oakleaf, frisée and corn
　　salad (mache)
Dressing (below)

TO SERVE
Salad (see ingredients)
Roast Salt and Pepper
　　(see p. 114)

Trim off the winglets from the duck. Remove any excess fat, then season with salt and black pepper and wrap in foil. Place the duck on a trivet in a large saucepan of boiling water, cover and steam for 2–2½ hours until tender. Carefully unwrap the foil covering the duck. Pour the cooking juices into a small bowl and reserve for the dressing.

Remove the legs and breasts from the duck carcass. Heat the groundnut oil in a frying-pan and fry the duck pieces skin-side down in it until they are crisp and brown. Drain on kitchen paper.

To serve, toss the salad leaves in half of the dressing and arrange a portion in the centre of a plate. Spoon a quarter of the remaining dressing on each plate. Set a duck leg and breast on each side of the salad. Serve the Roast Salt and Pepper separately.

DRESSING
1 teaspoon Dijon mustard
1 tablespoon white wine vinegar
2½ tablespoons groundnut oil
2½ tablespoons olive oil
1 teaspoon crème de cassis

1 tablespoon duck juice (see
　　main recipe)
salt and freshly ground black
　　pepper

Mix together the mustard and vinegar. Whisk in the groundnut and olive oils, then the crème de cassis and reserved duck juice. Season to taste with salt and black pepper.

*Shaun Hill's Artichoke Nissarda with
Hollandaise Sauce (page 116).*

Courgettes with Dill and Soured Cream

450 g (1 lb) courgettes, cut into matchsticks
salt and freshly ground black pepper
2 tablespoons groundnut oil
1 onion, chopped
1 clove garlic, crushed

1 tablespoon plain flour
300 ml (10 fl oz) soured cream
1 teaspoon white wine vinegar
2 tablespoons chopped dill
meat juices from pork (see main recipe)

Sprinkle the courgettes with 1 teaspoon salt. Leave for 30 minutes, then squeeze out the excess liquid. Blanch the courgettes in boiling, salted water. Drain. Heat the groundnut oil in a saucepan and gently fry the onion and garlic without colouring until tender. Stir in the flour and cook for a few seconds, then add the soured cream, vinegar and black pepper to taste. Stir in the courgettes, dill and meat juices from the pork.

When you are ready to serve, re-heat the courgettes, adding any extra meat juices. Season to taste with salt and black pepper.

❧ *Artichokes Nissarda* ❧
Hollandaise Sauce

Serves 4

4 large globe artichokes
juice of 1 lemon
1 teaspoon dried oregano

MUSHROOM STUFFING
1 tablespoon clarified butter
50 g (2 oz) shallots, finely chopped
100 g (4 oz) button mushrooms, chopped
salt and freshly ground black pepper

TO SERVE
Hollandaise Sauce (opposite)
chopped chives, to garnish (optional)

Ken Hom

BORN IN ARIZONA of Chinese parents, Ken Hom worked in his uncle's restaurant in Chicago from the age of eleven; and, although self-taught, he gave cookery lessons at night to pay his way through college. Today he is a sought-after food and restaurant consultant, cookery writer and international television cook – *Ken Hom's Chinese Cookery* was shown throughout the world.

Although his style is firmly based on the Chinese, he believes in making use of ingredients native to the country in which he is working. This has led to his unique blend of East and West, a marriage of the techniques, flavourings and inventiveness of the one and the produce of the other. The results include grilled lamb with sesame sauce, prawns with spicy South-East Asian pesto, and a wok-prepared vegetable stew spiked with ginger. Another major passion is cooking and eating for health.

Ken Hom with, from left: Rice Paper Prawn Rolls with Dipping Sauce (page 123), Wok-roasted Tuna with Spiced Confetti (page 126) and East-West Vegetarian Fried Rice (page 131).

❧ *Prawns with Spicy* ❧ *South-East Asian Pesto*

Serves 4–6 as a starter, 2–3 as a main course

12–18 fresh, uncooked large prawns
¼ teaspoon sea salt

¼ teaspoon freshly ground black pepper
1 tablespoon olive oil

TO SERVE
Spicy South-East Asian Pesto (below)
basil leaves, to garnish

4–6 bamboo skewers soaked in warm water for at least 10–15 minutes.

If you are going to barbecue the prawns, make a charcoal fire about 40 minutes before you are ready to cook so that the coals are ash-white. If you are using a grill, pre-heat it to high. Peel the prawns by removing the shell, legs and tail. Devein them by making a surface cut down the back of each prawn and removing the black, green or yellow intestine. Rinse well under cold, running water then pat dry thoroughly with kitchen paper. Season with the salt and pepper and moisten with the olive oil. Thread 3 prawns on to each bamboo skewer.

Make sure the coals are ash-white, then grill the prawns for 2–3 minutes on each side or until they are cooked to your taste. Alternatively, cook them on or under the pre-heated grill.

Drizzle the prawns with the Spicy South-East Asian Pesto and serve warm, garnished with basil leaves.

Spicy South-East Asian Pesto

3 tablespoons chopped Asian tropical basil (or traditional basil)
2 tablespoons chopped coriander leaves
2 tablespoons finely chopped garlic
1 tablespoon finely chopped fresh ginger

2 teaspoons finely chopped red chilli
2 teaspoons sea salt
½ teaspoon freshly ground black pepper
1 tablespoon olive oil
1 teaspoon sesame oil
2½ teaspoons groundnut oil
2 tablespoons lemon juice
3 tablespoons fish stock

Combine the ingredients in a food processor and blend until smooth.

🥠 *Rice Paper Prawn Rolls* 🥠
Dipping Sauce

Makes 10–15 spring rolls (depending on the size of the prawns)

225 g (8 oz) fresh, uncooked
   prawns, peeled and
   deveined (see main recipe
   opposite)
2 tablespoons sea salt
½ teaspoon salt
¼ teaspoon freshly ground black
   pepper
1 tablespoon olive oil (or oil
   from sun-dried tomatoes)

1 tablespoon tarragon leaves
2 tablespoons finely chopped
   chives
2 tablespoons finely chopped
   spring onions
2 tablespoons coarsely chopped
   sun-dried tomatoes, drained
Banh Trang rice-paper rounds
   (1 per prawn)
600 ml (1 pint) groundnut oil

TO SERVE
Dipping Sauce (see p. 124)

Fill a large bowl with cold water, add 1 tablespoon of the sea salt and gently wash the prawns in this water. Drain and repeat this process. Then rinse the prawns under cold, running water, drain and blot them dry with kitchen paper. Combine the prawns with the ½ teaspoon salt, pepper, olive oil, tarragon, chives, spring onions and sun-dried tomatoes. Mix well, cover and leave the mixture to marinate in the refrigerator for about 1 hour.

When you are ready to make the spring rolls, fill a large bowl with warm water. Dip a rice-paper round in the water and let it soften for a few seconds. Remove and drain on a clean tea-towel. Place 1 prawn and some of the marinade on the edge of 1 piece of the rice paper. Roll the edge of the paper over the prawn, fold in both ends and continue to roll to the end. The roll should be compact and tight, rather like a short, thick finger cigar about 7.5 cm (3 in) long. Set it on a clean plate and continue the process until you have used up all the prawns and marinade mixture.

Heat the groundnut oil in a wok or large frying-pan until it is moderately hot, about 350°F (175°C) on a thermometer, and fry the rolls a few at a time. They will tend to stick together, so don't try to separate them while cooking. Wait until the rolls are crisp, then remove them from the pan and separate them.

Drain on kitchen paper and serve at once with the Dipping Sauce.

Dipping Sauce

2 tablespoons fish sauce
2 tablespoons lime juice
4 tablespoons sugar

1–2 teaspoons chilli oil
2 tablespoons white rice vinegar

Combine all the ingredients together in a small bowl and mix well. Set aside for 10 minutes before serving.

🎀 *Prawns and Scallops* 🎀 *in Light Black Bean and Butter Sauce*

Serves 4

450 g (1 lb) fresh scallops, cleaned
450 g (1 lb) fresh, uncooked prawns, peeled and deveined (see main recipe, p. 122)
2 tablespoons sea salt
2 tablespoons olive oil
1 tablespoon black beans, coarsely chopped
1½ tablespoons finely chopped garlic
1 tablespoon finely chopped fresh ginger

2 tablespoons finely chopped shallots
1 tablespoon Chinese rice wine (or dry sherry)
1 tablespoon light soy sauce
120 ml (4 fl oz) fish stock
100 g (4 oz) peeled, de-seeded and coarsely chopped fresh tomatoes
2 tablespoons cold unsalted butter, cut into small pieces
a small handful of basil leaves, cut into strips

Separate the corals from the scallops and reserve. Fill a large bowl with cold water, add 1 tablespoon of the sea salt and gently wash the prawns in this water. Drain and repeat this process. Then rinse the prawns under cold, running water, drain and blot them dry with kitchen paper.

Heat half of the olive oil in a wok or large frying-pan. Add the prawns and scallops with their corals and stir-fry for 2 minutes. Remove with a slotted spoon and set aside. Wipe the wok clean with kitchen paper and re-heat. Add the remaining olive oil, then the beans, garlic, ginger and shallots. Stir-fry for 30 seconds.

Return the scallops and prawns to the wok, then add the rice wine, soy sauce and fish stock and cook over a high heat for 2–3 minutes. Add the chopped tomatoes, butter and basil and stir until they are warm.

Arrange the prawns and scallops on a platter and serve at once.

*Ken Hom's Prawns and Scallops in Light Black Bean
and Butter Sauce (opposite).*

🌸 *Wok-roasted Tuna* 🌸
Spiced Confetti

Serves 4

4 × 100 g (4 oz) tuna fillets,
    skinned
1½ tablespoons groundnut oil

MARINADE
1 tablespoon light soy sauce
1 tablespoon dark soy sauce

2 tablespoons Chinese rice wine
    (or dry sherry)
1 tablespoon sesame oil
1 teaspoon sea salt

TO SERVE
Spiced Confetti (below)
reduced chicken stock

small cooked vegetables of your
    choice such as baby pak
    choy, carrots or turnips, to
    garnish

Lay the tuna fillets on a platter. In a small bowl, combine the marinade ingredients and spoon this mixture evenly over the tuna. Leave the tuna to marinate for 2 hours in the refrigerator or for 1 hour at room temperature.

Heat a wok over high heat. When it is hot, add the groundnut oil. Remove the tuna fillets from the marinade and pat dry on kitchen paper. Add them to the hot wok and cook quickly on 1 side. Turn the fillets over and brown the other side. The tuna should remain medium-rare.

Transfer the tuna to warm plates and spoon the Spiced Confetti on top. Spoon a little reduced chicken stock around each portion, and garnish with vegetables.

Spiced Confetti

1½ tablespoons olive oil
2 tablespoons finely chopped
    garlic
1 tablespoon finely chopped
    fresh ginger
1 tablespoon finely chopped
    shallots
3 tablespoons finely chopped
    spring onions
1 tablespoon de-seeded, finely
    chopped red chilli
4 tablespoons finely chopped
    carrots

4 tablespoons finely chopped
    courgettes
2 tablespoons finely chopped
    red pepper
1 teaspoon ground cumin
1 teaspoon five-peppercorn
    mixture, ground
1 teaspoon salt
1 teaspoon sugar
1 tablespoon finely chopped
    coriander leaves

Heat a wok until it is hot. Add the olive oil, garlic, ginger, shallots, spring onions and chilli and stir-fry for 30 seconds. Add the carrots, courgettes and peppers and continue to stir-fry for 1 minute. Finally, add the cumin, peppercorn mixture, salt, sugar and coriander and continue to stir-fry for another minute. Transfer to a dish and keep warm.

❧ Steamed Salmon in ❧ Chinese Leaves
Orange and Lemon Sauce

Serves 4

4 × 100 g (4 oz) salmon fillets, skinned

4 large Chinese leaves, blanched

1 teaspoon sea salt plus extra for seasoning

1 teaspoon roasted and ground Szechuan peppercorns, sieved

TO SERVE
Orange and Lemon Sauce (below)

Place each fillet of salmon on one end of a cabbage leaf. Sprinkle with the sea salt and Szechuan peppercorns. Roll up each leaf, folding in the sides as you go to encase the pieces of salmon. Set the fish on a plate in a steamer over simmering water and cook for 8–10 minutes until just firm to the touch. The juices will be added to the Orange and Lemon Sauce.

To serve, pour some Orange and Lemon Sauce over each piece of cabbage-wrapped fish and serve at once.

Orange and Lemon Sauce

1½ tablespoons finely chopped shallots

2 teaspoons finely chopped fresh ginger

2 tablespoons Chinese rice wine (or dry sherry)

6 tablespoons fish stock

1 tablespoon lemon juice

1 tablespoon orange juice

fish juices (see main recipe)

25 g (1 oz) cold butter, cut into small pieces

freshly ground black pepper

2 teaspoons finely chopped coriander leaves

2 teaspoons finely chopped chives

Place the shallots and ginger in a small saucepan and heat gently to remove the moisture. Add the rice wine and cook over high heat until it has evaporated, then add the fish stock and the lemon and orange juice. Pour off the fish juices that have collected in the salmon plate and add to the saucepan. Reduce the liquid by half by fast boiling, then stir in the butter, a few pieces at a time. Season to taste with sea salt and black pepper. Add the coriander and chives and cook for 30 seconds.

❧ *Multi-Spiced Crispy Poussin* ❧

Serves 4

2 × 550–750 g (1¼–1½ lb) poussins
25 g (1 oz) plain flour

900 ml (1½ pints) groundnut oil for deep-frying

MARINADE
1 teaspoon five-spice powder
2 tablespoons sea salt
1 teaspoon Szechuan peppercorns, roasted, finely ground and sieved

2 tablespoons finely chopped orange rind
1 teaspoon freshly ground five peppercorn mixture
1 tablespoon dried thyme

TO SERVE
lemon wedges

Split each poussin along either side of the backbone and discard the bone. Trim off the knuckle end of the drumsticks. Make a small slit in the pointed end of each breast and tuck the end of a drumstick into each one to give a flat shape. Pat the poussin dry with a kitchen towel.

Mix the marinade ingredients together in a bowl. Rub the marinade evenly on the poussins and marinate for about 2 hours. Remove the poussins from the marinade. Lightly dust the poussins with the flour, shaking off any excess.

Heat the oil in a large saucepan or deep-fryer to about 350°C (175°F) and deep-fry the poussins, turning once until they are golden-brown. This will take about 20–25 minutes. Drain on kitchen paper. Test with a skewer through the thickest part of the meat to make sure it is cooked. The juices should run clear.

Serve with lemon wedges.

🦢 *Grilled Lamb* 🦢
Sesame Sauce, Green Salad

Serves 4

4 × 175 g (6 oz) pieces lean lamb
    fillet, cut from the eye of
    the loin.

MARINADE
1½ tablespoons sesame oil
2 teaspoons light soy sauce
1 teaspoon salt
½ teaspoon freshly ground
    black pepper
1 tablespoon dried thyme

TO SERVE
Sesame Sauce (below)
Green Salad (see p. 130)

Trim the meat completely of any fat.

Mix the marinade ingredients together in a small bowl. Rub the lamb fillet thoroughly with the marinade. Allow the meat to marinate for at least 2 hours at room temperature, or longer in the refrigerator.

Make a charcoal fire and, when the coals are hot, grill the lamb for about 10 minutes on each side – less if you prefer the meat pink. Alternatively, pre-heat a grill to high and cook the meat on or under it. Remove the lamb from the heat and leave it to rest on a warm plate for at least 20 minutes. Any juices should be reserved for use in the Sesame Sauce.

Thinly slice the lamb fillet and arrange on individual plates. Pour on the Sesame Sauce. Serve with Green Salad.

Sesame Sauce

150 ml (5 fl oz) chicken stock
3 tablespoons sesame paste (or
    creamy peanut butter)
2 tablespoons Japanese rice wine
    (mirin)
1 tablespoon Japanese white rice
    vinegar

½ teaspoon freshly ground black
    pepper
1 teaspoon sea salt
lamb juices (see main recipe)
2 tablespoons finely chopped
    spring onions

Simmer the chicken stock in a saucepan, then whisk in the sesame paste until smooth. Add the rice wine and white rice vinegar and season with the salt and pepper. Stir in any juices from the lamb with the spring onions, and warm gently.

Clive Howe

AFTER SEVEN YEARS with Anton Mosimann at The Dorchester, and a stint at Rookery Hall in Nantwich, Clive Howe is cooking in the heart of the Cotswolds, at the 500-year-old *Lygon Arms*. Surrounded by the best of British produce, much of which is in the gardens of the *Lygon Arms*, he has developed a cookery style and menu that explore the very best of British fare, including classics like braised shank of venison and haricot of Cotswold lamb, and deeply traditional desserts such as orange flower water and honey curd tarts. This, he says, is 'proper cooking'.

Like most top-flight chefs, he became passionate about food when very young, and has worked in hotels since he was fourteen. His principal hobby, one he shares with his Swiss mentor, is collecting old cookery books. He considers it a great challenge to bring to life a 200-year-old recipe, reinterpreting it with modern ingredients. In doing so, he has helped to demonstrate that modern British cooking can be second to none.

Clive Howe with, clockwise from left: Braised Shank of Venison in Beer and Onion Gravy with vegetables (page 144), Roast Cornish Sea Bass and Scallops with Parsley Sauce (page 137) and Orange Flower Water and Honey Curd Tart with Orange Sauce and Caramelised Orange Peel (page 147).

Elderberry Sauce

100 g (4 oz) elderberries
300 ml (10 fl oz) game stock
25 g (1 oz) redcurrant jelly
100 ml (3½ fl oz) red wine

2 tablespoons ruby port
salt and freshly ground black
    pepper
15 g (½ oz) unsalted butter

Place 75 g (3 oz) of the elderberries in a saucepan with the stock, redcurrant jelly, red wine and port. Bring to the boil and boil rapidly to reduce by half. Pass through a fine sieve into a clean saucepan. Add the remaining elderberries and simmer for 2 minutes. Season to taste with salt and black pepper and whisk in the butter.

❧ *Hotch-Potch of* ❧ *Devonshire Squab Pigeon*

Serves 4

100 g (4 oz) cooked pearl barley
    (approx. 40–50 g/ 1½–2 oz
    uncooked)
75 g (3 oz) dried apricots, soaked
    until soft and cut into
    julienne strips
25 g (1 oz) mixed parsley,
    tarragon and thyme,
    chopped
salt and freshly ground black
    pepper
4 squab pigeons, boned
2 tablespoons olive oil

750 ml (1¼ pints) strong stock
    (made with squabs' bones)
16 button onions
16 young carrots
50 g (2 oz) baby leeks, cut into
    5 cm (2 in) lengths
100 g (4 oz) mixed wild
    mushrooms
16 asparagus tips, peeled
100 g (4 oz) Savoy cabbage, cut
    into 2.5 cm (1 in) squares
a pinch of saffron

Clive Howe's Hotch-Potch of Devonshire
Squab Pigeon (above).

Bruno Loubet

A T ONLY THIRTY years of age, French-born Bruno Loubet is
chef de cuisine of the *Four Seasons Restaurant* at London's Inn
on the Park, for which he has won a Michelin star. Born near
Bordeaux, he wanted to be a chef from the age of six; by fourteen he
was working in local restaurants on days off from school, learning
about charcuterie and pâtisserie. After catering school and national
service (during which he also cooked), he came to London. There he
worked at Tante Claire then, to great acclaim, at Gastronome One,
followed by Raymond Blanc's Manoir and Le Petit Blanc in Oxford.

His love for food was born through his grandmother and his main
emphasis is still on regional French and classical bourgeois cooking.
His dishes use humble ingredients – virtually his trademark – combined with modern and current touches of refinement and great
sophistication. Many of these touches are inspired by his adoptive city
and its international influences: for example, the use of Indian and
Chinese spices, such as cardamom and star anise, in a sauce for lamb.
No follower of trends, he believes above all in pure earthy flavours,
as well as in top-quality ingredients.

---

*Bruno Loubet with, clockwise from left: Peppers with
Salt Cod and Lobster Filling with Lobster Pepper
Sauce and Garlic Sauce (page 153), Poached Lamb
Fillets with Couscous and Spicy Pumpkin (page 157)
and Mackerel and Scallop Kebabs with Tomato Relish
and Onion Rings (page 154).*

Remove the lamb fillets from the bones and trim off the fat. Chop the bones and place in a saucepan. Add the carrots, onions and celery with the tomatoes and thyme. Cover with 1.5 litres (2½ pints) water. Bring to the boil and simmer, uncovered, for 1 hour. Strain, then pass this stock through a fine sieve into a clean saucepan and keep hot. Place the lamb fillets in just enough of the hot stock to cover and simmer, covered, for about 8 minutes. Remove the meat from stock, cover and leave to rest in a warm place until ready to serve.

Boil 600 ml (1 pint) of the lamb stock to reduce it to 150 ml (5 fl oz). Blend in a food processor with the butter and olive oil for 30 seconds, then season with salt and black pepper.

To serve, spoon Couscous into the centre of each plate and garnish with the Spicy Pumpkin and its spices. Sprinkle with chopped coriander leaves. Top with slices of lamb and the sauce made from the lamb stock.

Couscous

200 g (7 oz) couscous
hot lamb stock (see main recipe)

salt and freshly ground black pepper
2 tablespoons pumpkin liquid (see Spicy Pumpkin below)

Put the couscous in a bowl and add 100 ml (3½ fl oz) of the hot lamb stock. Season and mix well. Leave to swell for 5 minutes. Repeat the process twice, seasoning only if necessary. Add the pumpkin liquid to the couscous, cover and place over a low heat to keep warm.

Spicy Pumpkin

2 star anise
1 teaspoon caraway seeds
2 cardamon pods, crushed
50 g (2 oz) root ginger, grated
1 chilli, cut into fine rings

grated rind of 1 lemon
450 g (1 lb) wedge of pumpkin, peeled and cut into 2 cm (¾ in) squares

Place the spices in a saucepan with the lemon rind and pumpkin. Just cover with some of the lamb stock and add a pinch of salt. Simmer, covered, for 5–10 minutes until the pumpkin is tender. Drain off the cooking liquid, reserving 2 tablespoons for the couscous.

Bruno Loubet's Celeriac and Ceps Terrine with
Parsley Sauce (page 162).

Roast Turkey Breast Studded with Parma Ham and Garlic
Mixed Vegetables

Serves 6–8

6 cloves garlic, quartered
salt and freshly ground black
 pepper
1 thick slice Parma ham (approx.
 150 g/5 oz), sliced into 5 cm
 (2 in) lardons

2.75 kg (6 lb) oven-ready turkey
 breast
1 tablespoon oil
½ tablespoon tomato purée
100 ml (3½ fl oz) white wine
2 tablespoons soy sauce
25 g (1 oz) unsalted butter

PARSLEY BUTTER
150 g (5 oz) unsalted butter
50 g (2 oz) blanched, chopped
 parsley

TO SERVE
Mixed Vegetables (opposite)
sauce (see main recipe)

Pre-heat the oven to gas mark 6, 400°F (200°C).

For the parsley butter, blend together the butter with the parsley. This can be done in a food processor or by hand.

To prepare the turkey for the oven, first remove the wishbone, then, with your hands, carefully detach the skin from the meat and pull back the skin from the breast. With a sharp knife, make some deep incisions in the breast. Dip the garlic quarters in salt and black pepper, then insert the garlic and the lardons of Parma ham in the incisions in the meat. Spread the parsley butter over the turkey breast, then pull the skin back into place. Secure the bird with string.

Place in a roasting tin with 2 glasses of water. Brush the bird with the olive oil, cover with foil and roast in the oven for about 2 hours. Remove the foil towards the end of cooking in order to brown the skin. When the turkey is cooked, remove it from the oven. Transfer it to a plate and leave to rest in a warm place.

Pour all the fat off the liquid in the roasting tin and place the tin and the remaining juices on top of the stove. Add the tomato purée, white wine, 450 ml (15 fl oz) water and the soy sauce. Boil for about 15 minutes until the liquid has reduced to a thin sauce consistency, then stir in the butter and adjust the seasoning. Pass the sauce through a fine sieve.

To serve, place the turkey in the centre of a large plate and arrange all the Mixed Vegetables around it. Serve the sauce separately.

Mixed Vegetables
450 g (1 lb) carrots
500 g (1¼ lb) celeriac
450 g (1 lb) parsnips
350 g (12 oz) button onions
100 g (4 oz) unsalted butter
2 small glasses white wine (or
    water)
100 ml (3½ fl oz) vinegar
salt and freshly ground black
    pepper

Cut the carrots, celeriac and parsnips in even-sized chunks. In a roasting tin on top of the stove sauté them with the button onions in the butter until golden. Add the wine and vinegar to the tin and let the liquid bubble rapidly. Season generously with salt and black pepper and place in the oven to roast with the turkey for 30–45 minutes until tender.

❧ *Mushrooms and Chestnuts* ❧
en Cocotte

Serves 4

about 24 Spanish chestnut
    leaves, soaked overnight if
    dried
200 g (7 oz) chestnuts
65 g (2½ oz) unsalted butter
100 g (4 oz) shallots, thinly sliced
350 g (12 oz) mixed wild
    mushrooms and field
    mushrooms – choose from
    button, pied de mouton,
    chanterelles, oyster and
    black trumpet

½ clove garlic, crushed
1 tablespooon chopped parsley
1 tablespoon chopped tarragon
4 tablespoons Madeira
salt and freshly ground black
    pepper
about 100 g (4 oz) puff pastry
beaten egg

Pre-heat the oven to gas mark 9, 475°F (240°C).

Wash and dry the chestnut leaves. Make a small incision in each chestnut. Cook the chestnuts in boiling water for about 30 minutes until soft inside, then peel away both the inner and outer skins.

Melt 25 g (1 oz) of the butter in a small saucepan and cook the shallots

Wash the rice in a sieve under cold, running water, then place in a heavy-based saucepan with the milk, 50 g (2 oz) sugar, vanilla pod and orange rind. Bring to simmering point, then cook, covered, very slowly for about 1½ hours. Stir in the cream and cook, covered, for a further 15 minutes. Remove the vanilla pod and orange rind and pass the rice through a sieve to separate the creamy rice from the liquid. Chill the liquid until required.

Mix the brioche crumbs and nibbed almonds. Using floured hands, shape the rice into 8 balls. Dip in the egg beaten with a pinch of sugar, then in the brioche and almond mixture. Repeat once more to give a good coating. Deep-fry the rice croquettes in hot oil until crisp and golden. Drain on absorbent paper.

To serve, stick a piece of angelica and a sprig of mint in each croquette and dust with icing sugar. Pour a little of the creamy rice liquid in the centre of each plate and arrange 2 rice croquettes on the liquid. Pour some Raspberry Coulis around the liquid and draw a cocktail stick through the sauces where they join to give a decorative effect. Serve immediately.

Raspberry Coulis
150 g (5 oz) raspberries
50 g (2 oz) icing sugar

Liquidise the raspberries, sugar and 3 tablespoons water together and pass through a fine sieve.

✣ *Chocolate Tartlets* ✣
Blackberry Coulis, Crème Fraiche

Makes 4

PASTRY
50 g (2 oz) unsalted butter, softened
40 g (1½ oz) caster sugar
½ beaten egg

½ teaspoon finely grated orange rind
75 g (3 oz) plain flour

CHOCOLATE FILLING
3 egg yolks
25 g (1 oz) caster sugar
100 g (4 oz) unsalted butter, melted

150 g (5 oz) dark chocolate, melted
1 egg white
a pinch of salt

TO SERVE
icing sugar for dusting
4 sprigs of mint, to decorate
Blackberry Coulis (below)

crème fraiche, thinned to a thick
pouring consistency with
milk

For the pastry, mix the butter, caster sugar, egg and orange rind together, then quickly mix in the flour to give a soft dough. Wrap in cling film and leave in the refrigerator for 2 hours.

Pre-heat the oven to gas mark 4, 350°F (180°C).

On a lightly floured surface, roll out the dough to a thickness of 3 mm (⅛ in) and use to line 4 × 10 cm (4 in) tartlet tins. Cover the pastry in the tins with foil or greaseproof paper cut to fit and weighed down with dried beans. Bake blind for 5 minutes, then carefully remove the beans and cook for a further 5 minutes. Leave to cool.

For the chocolate filling, whisk the egg yolks and caster sugar with 2 tablespoons water until pale and fluffy, then stir in the melted butter and chocolate. Whisk the egg white with a pinch of salt until stiff, then fold into the chocolate mixture. Use to fill the tartlets. Bake for 6 minutes until lightly set.

To serve, unmould the tartlets and dust each one with icing sugar and decorate with a sprig of mint. Place each tartlet on a large plate and pour Blackberry Coulis on one side of the plate and crème fraiche on the other. Using a cocktail stick, draw a pattern through the sauces on both sides of the plate where they join to give a decorative effect.

Blackberry Coulis
150 g (5 oz) blackberries
50 g (2 oz) sugar
50 ml (2 fl oz) orange juice

Combine the blackberries, sugar, orange juice and 50 ml (2 fl oz) water in a saucepan and bring to the boil. Liquidise then pass through a fine sieve.

Paul and Jeanne Rankin

WITH A BACKGROUND of good home cooking, absorbed from his mother and aunt, Irish-born Paul Rankin first entered the profession as a waiter. The decision to become a chef was taken when he and Jeanne, his Canadian wife, were travelling around the world and planning their future. (They bought their first cookery book in Katmandu.) Both went on to train with Albert Roux – Paul at Le Gavroche, Jeanne at Le Poulbot and Gavvers. After a year in Vancouver in Canada they moved to California, to the Mountview Hotel in the Napa Valley. They returned to Ireland two and a half years later to open their own restaurant, *Roscoff*, in Belfast. In doing so, they have acquired the first Michelin star in the province.

The Rankin style is basically modern French, but it displays strong influences from America and the Orient. In the warmth of California, Paul and Jeanne were led towards lighter ingredients and interpretations; eating out in Hong Kong, Vancouver and San Francisco – the cities with the best Chinese food in the world – introduced them to the potential of allying Eastern ideas to their own inventiveness.

Paul and Jeanne Rankin with, clockwise from left:
Trio of Chicken Roscoff with Mixed Vegetables and
Beurre Fondue (page 170), Roast Bananas in Puff Pastry
with Chocolate Sauce (page 184) and Baked Goat's
Cheese with Roast Beetroot (page 175).

Steamed Goujonettes of Monkfish
Dressing, Red Pepper Garnish

Serves 4

450–600 g (1–1¼ lb) monkfish
    fillet, well trimmed
4 leeks
plain flour

oil for deep-frying
salt and freshly ground black
    pepper

TO SERVE
Dressing (below)
Red Pepper Garnish (opposite)
black and white sesame seeds
    dry-roasted in a frying-pan

Cut the monkfish into 20 even-sized pieces about 7.5 cm (3 in) long and 2 cm (¾ in) wide.

Cut down the side of each leek and release the individual layers. Cut 20 ribbons of leek to wrap around the fish. Blanch the ribbons in boiling salted water, then drain them and refresh them in cold water. Cut the leek that remains after making the ribbons into julienne strips and toss them in flour. Shake off excess flour. Heat the oil and deep-fry the leek strips until crisp and golden. Drain on absorbent paper.

Season the fish with salt and black pepper and wrap a leek ribbon around each one. Steam the goujonettes for 4–5 minutes until just firm to the touch.

To serve, spoon some Dressing on to each warm plate and arrange 5 goujonettes around the edge. Pile the leek julienne strips in the centre of each portion, and a little Red Pepper Garnish between each piece of fish. Sprinkle with sesame seeds and serve at once.

Dressing

50 ml (2 fl oz) sesame oil
50 ml (2 fl oz) groundnut oil
2 tablespoons rice wine vinegar
2 tablespoons mushroom soy
    sauce
1 tablespoon finely chopped
    Chinese pickled ginger

Whisk all the ingredients together.

Red Pepper Garnish
4 red peppers, de-seeded
6 tablespoons rice wine vinegar
4 tablespoons sugar

Cut the peppers into quarters and trim them into neat oblongs. Cut each oblong into thin strips, then place the strips in a saucepan with 200 ml (7 fl oz) water and the vinegar and sugar. Simmer until tender and glazed. Leave to cool.

❧ *Stuffed Quail* ❧
Buttered Risotto

Serves 4

salt and freshly ground black pepper	8 quail, boned
	25 g (1 oz) butter

STUFFING
100 g (4 oz) chicken livers	1 small clove garlic, chopped
milk	25 g (1 oz) bacon, diced
15 g (½ oz) dried ceps	1 tablespoon toasted pine
225 g (8 oz) fresh spinach leaves, blanched and squeezed dry	kernels
50 g (2 oz) unsalted butter	salt and freshly ground black
1 small shallot, chopped	pepper

TO SERVE
Buttered Risotto (see p. 170)	sautéd wild mushrooms
chicken gravy	sprigs of parsley, thyme or sage
cooked broad beans, skinned	

First make the stuffing. Cover the chicken livers with milk and leave to one side. Cover the ceps with boiling water and leave to one side for 30 minutes. Drain the livers, and drain and chop the ceps. Chop the spinach. Heat half of the butter in a frying-pan and cook the shallot, garlic, bacon and ceps in it until lightly browned. Set aside. Heat the remaining butter in another pan and cook the chicken livers in it until well browned on all sides. Remove them from the pan, then add the spinach to the pan juices and sauté quickly. Chop the chicken livers. Combine the shallot mixture with the chicken livers, spinach and pine kernels. Season to taste with salt and black pepper.

Pre-heat the oven to gas mark 8, 450°F (230°C).

Season the insides of the quails, then fill each one with one-eighth of the stuffing. Neaten the shape of the birds and secure with string, if wished.

Heat the butter in a roasting tin and set the quails in the tin. Roast for about 15 minutes. If wished, grill the quails a little on each side to give a slight barbecue flavour. Keep warm until the risotto is ready to serve.

To serve, spoon some Buttered Risotto into the centre of each warm plate and set 2 quails on top. Spoon a little chicken gravy around each portion, and garnish with the broad beans, sautéd wild mushrooms and a sprig of herbs.

Buttered Risotto

40 g (1½ oz) unsalted butter
1 small onion, chopped
100 g (4 oz) arborio rice

600 ml (1 pt) chicken stock
salt and freshly ground black pepper

Heat one-third of the butter in a saucepan and sauté the onion until soft. Add the rice and stir until each grain is moistened with butter. Add the stock a ladle at a time and simmer, stirring frequently, until all the stock is used up and the rice is tender. Stir in the remaining butter and season to taste.

❧ Trio of Chicken Roscoff ❧
Mixed Vegetables, Beurre Fondue

Serves 4

1 × 1.5 kg (3½ lb) chicken
1 bottle red wine
1 sprig of thyme
1 bay leaf
4 black peppercorns
2 tablespoons oil
25 g (1 oz) carrot, chopped
25 g (1 oz) onion, chopped

25 g (1 oz) celery, chopped
1 clove garlic, chopped
900 ml (1½ pints) chicken stock
2 teaspoons tomato purée
salt and freshly ground black pepper
15 g (½ oz) unsalted butter

STUFFING
15 g (½ oz) unsalted butter
25 g (1 oz) veal sweetbreads, blanched and diced (or chicken liver, diced)
1 small onion, chopped

25 g (1 oz) mushrooms, chopped
25 g (1 oz) spinach leaves
1 sprig of tarragon, chopped
salt and freshly ground black pepper

TO SERVE
Mixed vegetables (opposite)
Beurre Fondue (see p. 172)

Remove the drumsticks from the chicken with a sharp knife and cut off the end of each one to expose the bone. Remove and bone the thighs. Remove the wings and cut off the wing tips. Remove the breasts from the carcass. Reserve all the bone trimmings and carcass for the sauce. Store the thighs and breasts in the refrigerator until needed.

Combine the red wine with the thyme, bay leaf and peppercorns and pour it over the drumsticks and wings. Allow them to marinate for up to 24 hours. Remove from the liquid and pat dry. Reserve the marinade.

Pre-heat the oven to gas mark 6, 400°F (200°C).

Heat the oil in a large, heavy saucepan and brown the carcass and bone trimmings, drumsticks and wings in it. Add the carrot, onion, celery and garlic and cook for a few minutes, then add the reserved marinade, 600 ml (1 pt) of the stock and the tomato purée. Bring to the boil then simmer, uncovered, for 45 minutes until the drumsticks and wings are tender. Remove the drumsticks and wings, then strain the sauce into a clean pan and boil rapidly to reduce to a syrupy consistency. Season to taste with salt and black pepper. Return the drumsticks and wings to the sauce and warm gently.

For the stuffing, heat the butter in a saucepan and sweat all the ingredients except the salt and pepper in it, then blend them in a food processor. Season. Season the thighs and fill them with the stuffing. Wrap tightly in foil and bake for 20 minutes. Leave to rest for 5 minutes before opening. Season the chicken breasts then, using a roasting tin or ovenproof frying-pan, fry them, skin-side down, in 15 g (½ oz) of the unsalted butter for 5–10 minutes until the skin is crisp and golden. Transfer to the oven for a further 10–15 minutes until cooked. Keep warm.

To serve, arrange a drumstick or wing on each plate on a small portion of mashed potato. Cut the breasts in half and arrange each piece on a small bed of spinach. Cut each thigh into 4 medallions and place 2 on a small amount of carrot. Spoon some red wine sauce around the plate and garnish with glazed onions, mushrooms and lardons. Spoon a little Beurre Fondue over the chicken breast and garnish with a sprig of chervil.

Mixed Vegetables

225 g (8 oz) potatoes, peeled
90 g (3½ oz) unsalted butter
salt and freshly ground black
    pepper
2 carrots, shredded
sugar
50 g (2 oz) tiny button onions,
    peeled

50 g (2 oz) tiny button
    mushrooms
25 g (1 oz) bacon lardons
225 g (8 oz) tender young
    spinach leaves
4 sprigs of chervil

Cook the potatoes in boiling, salted water for about 20 minutes, then drain and mash them with 25 g (1 oz) of the butter. Season to taste. Place the carrots in a small saucepan with 15 g (½ oz) of the butter, a pinch of sugar and salt and just cover them with some of the remaining chicken stock. Cook uncovered, until tender and glazed. Place the onions in a small saucepan with 15 g (½ oz) of the butter and a pinch of sugar and just cover them with the remaining stock. Cook uncovered, for 10–15 minutes until tender and glazed. Pan-fry the mushrooms in 15 g (½ oz) of the butter until golden. Pan-fry the lardons in 15 g (½ oz) of the butter until golden. Blanch the spinach and sauté it in 15 g (½ oz) of the butter.

Beurre Fondue
1 tablespoon double cream
25 g (1 oz) unsalted butter
lemon juice
salt and freshly ground black
  pepper

Warm the cream in a small saucepan then take it off the heat and whisk in the butter to make a creamy sauce – the butter must not melt. Adjust the seasoning with the lemon juice and salt and black pepper.

Noisettes of Lamb with a Herb and Olive Crust

Serves 4

2 racks of lamb – ask your
  butcher for any trimmings
100 g (4 oz) onion, chopped
salt and freshly ground black
  pepper
100 g (4 oz) celery
100 g (4 oz) carrot, chopped
3 cloves garlic, chopped
1 litre (1¾ pints) chicken stock
2 tablespoons olive oil (or
  groundnut oil)

65 g (2½ oz) unsalted butter
1 chicken breast, skinned and
  boned
1 egg white
50 g (2 oz) stoned black olives
1 tablespoon each finely
  chopped parsley, rosemary
  and thyme
120 ml (4 fl oz) double cream
25 g (1 oz) breadcrumbs (or
  brioche crumbs)

TO SERVE
potato gratin
braised fennel

sprigs of parsley, thyme or sage,
  to garnish

Pre-heat the oven to gas mark 8, 450°F (230°C).

Peel the skin off the racks of lamb and trim all the meat from between the bones. Cut each rack into 4 pieces, then cut away the bones as necessary to leave 8 thick cutlets of lamb with a single bone on each. Lightly bet out each cutlet, and season with salt and black pepper. Discard the fat, but reserve all the bones and trimmings. Place the trimmings in a roasting tin with the chopped onion, celery and carrot and 2 cloves of the garlic. Roast for 1 hour, turning occasionally until well browned. Drain off the excess fat, then transfer the trimmings to a large saucepan and add the chicken stock. Simmer for 1 hour, then pass through a fine sieve. Reserve.

Meanwhile, heat the oil and 25 g (1 oz) of the butter in a roasting tin or ovenproof frying-pan until very hot, then quickly brown the cutlets of lamb in it on both sides. Remove the cutlets from the pan and leave to go cold. Keep the pan to one side.

In a food processor, blend the chicken and egg white until smooth, then pulse in the olives, the remaining garlic and half of the herbs. With the machine running, add the cream to give a thick mousse. Season generously. Spread a little of the mousse on to each cold cutlet, then press in breadcrumbs to just cover the mousse. Sprinkle with the remaining herbs.

Pre-heat the oven to gas mark 8, 450°F (230°C) again. On top of the stove, melt 25 g (1 oz) of the remaining butter in the roasting tin or frying-pan you used for the cutlets. Set the cutlets in it, mousse-side up, and roast in the oven for 5 minutes. Turn the cutlets over and roast for a further 5–7 minutes, depending on how pink you like your lamb.

Bring the reserved lamb stock to the boil and, if necessary, boil rapidly to reduce it to a thin gravy consistency. Whisk in the remaining butter.

Serve 2 cutlets per person, with a little of the lamb stock poured around each portion. Garnish with a sprig of herbs. Serve with potato gratin and braised fennel.

caramel colour. Pour about three-quarters of the caramel over the apples and cook in the oven for about 10 minutes until just tender, stirring occasionally. Leave to go cold. Reserve the remaining caramel if you are making Toffee Sauce.

Reduce the oven temperature to gas mark 4, 350°F (180°C). Bake the pastry cases blind for about 20 minutes until golden, removing the beans after 10 minutes. Leave to go cold, then unmould the pastry from the cases.

For the crumble, pulse all the ingredients together lightly in a food processor until of 'pea-size' consistency.

Fill each pastry tart with 4–5 apple wedges, then sprinkle with the crumble mix. Place them under a pre-heated grill and cook for 5 minutes until golden. Alternatively, bake the tarts at gas mark 5, 375°F (190°C) for about 15 minutes. To serve, place the tarts on individual plates, dust with icing sugar and decorate with sprigs of mint. Serve with warm Toffee Sauce or crème fraiche.

Toffee Sauce
reserved caramel (see main
     recipe)
150 ml (5 fl oz) double cream

Warm the caramel gently in a saucepan, then stir in the double cream. Heat gently, stirring, until all the caramel is dissolved and you have a smooth sauce.

*Paul and Jeanne Rankin's Lemon and Passion Fruit
Mousse with Kiwi Wedges (page 182).*

(This mixture will keep in the refrigerator for several days and is sufficient for 8 portions. Any leftover mixture can be spread on toast and grilled.)

For the fish, pre-heat the oven to gas mark 6, 400°F (200°C). Skin each piece of fish and cover with one-eighth of the cheese mixture, spread in an even layer. Place on an oiled or buttered baking tray. Cook under a grill pre-heated to medium-high for 5–6 minutes, then transfer to the oven for 2 minutes to finish cooking.

To serve, set a portion of fish on each plate. Arrange the tomatoes around the fish. Drizzle with Vinaigrette Dressing and sprinkle with chopped chives.

❧ *Confit of Duck* ❧
Braised Butter Beans

Serves 4

4 duck legs
about 2 kg (4½ lb) duck or
    goose fat (or beef
    dripping), melted
4 tablespoons clear honey

MARINADE
a few sprigs of thyme
3 bay leaves
12 black peppercorns
6 basil leaves, shredded
1 clove garlic, thinly sliced
2 shallots, chopped
1 cm (½ in) piece root ginger,
    sliced

1 teaspoon Worcestershire
    sauce
1 teaspoon soy sauce
1 teaspoon balsamic vinegar
1 tablespoon white wine
1 tablespoon olive oil

TO SERVE
Braised Butter Beans
    (see p. 194)
75 g (3 oz) curly endive
Vinaigrette Dressing
    (see p. 188)
gravy (optional)

Gary Rhodes' Haddock and Welsh Rarebit (page 191).

Ruth Rogers and
Rose Gray

THE *River Café* in Hammersmith began life as canteen for the offices of architect Richard Rogers. Now his wife Ruth and her partner Rose Gray have turned it into a fully fledged, and highly fashionable, restaurant that serves regional Italian food. Neither has any formal training, but learned through living in Italy, frequent visits to that country and the tutelage of Ruth's mother-in-law, who comes from Florence.

Their style, a sophisticated reinterpretation of classical recipes mainly from northern Italy and Tuscany, relies primarily on simple methods and seasonal, fresh produce. Char-grilling and quick pan-frying are common, as is the slower all-in-one pot cooking, *integame*. In their quest for nothing but the best, Ruth and Rose have imported seeds — of cavolo nero, a black Italian cabbage, and many Italian herbs — which are organically grown for them; large rosemary bushes flourish at the café itself; and there is now a café allotment which will be cultivated by their team of young chefs. Sources in Italy are plundered for the very best olive oils fresh from the press, bread flours, polenta, Italian salted capers and anchovies and other seasonings.

Rose Gray and Ruth Rogers with, from left: Polenta (page 206), Mushroom Risotto (page 205) and Whole Marinated Sea Bass Char-grilled then Baked, with Salsa Verde (page 207).

Pre-heat the oven to gas mark 5, 375°F (190°C).

Wash and dry the sea bass. Put salt and pepper and half of the fennel seeds in the belly cavity. Grill the fish on each side on a medium-hot griddle or barbecue until the skin is charred – about 15 minutes in all. Transfer the fish to a large ovenproof dish with the remaining fennel seeds, onions, fennel slices, lemon slices, parsley stalks and bay leaves. Pour over the lemon juice, olive oil and wine. Bake for about 25 minutes, until the fish is firm to the touch. Serve the sea bass whole with Salsa Verde.

Salsa Verde

3–4 tablespoons basil leaves
3–4 tablespoons flat-leaf parsley leaves
50 g (2 oz) salted capers, washed
50 g (2 oz) salted anchovies, washed and boned (or tinned anchovy fillets)
1 clove garlic, chopped
1 tablespoon red wine vinegar
1–2 tablespoons Dijon mustard (optional)
salt and freshly ground black pepper

Pulse the herbs, capers, anchovies and garlic together in a food processor. Transfer the mixture to a bowl and stir in the vinegar, oil and mustard if wished. Season to taste with salt and black pepper.

❧ Pan-fried Chicken ❧ Stuffed with Mascarpone and Rosemary

Serves 2

2 tablespoons rosemary leaves, plus a few extra sprigs
8 tablespoons mascarpone
salt and freshly ground black pepper
1.5 kg (3 lb) oven-ready chicken, boned, the drumsticks discarded
1 tablespoon olive oil
2 tablespoons white wine

Ruth Rogers' and Rose Gray's Pan-fried Calves Liver with Balsamic Vinegar and Crème Fraiche, served with Braised Cavalo Nero (page 211).

Slice 2 of the garlic cloves and halve the rest. Make incisions in the pork and press the garlic slices into the gaps. Season generously with salt and black pepper.

Heat the oil in a wide, shallow saucepan, then add the pork and brown it well on all sides. Pour off the oil from the pan. Pour the milk over the meat and add the remaining garlic and the lemon rind. Simmer gently, uncovered, for 1½–2 hours, turning the meat from time to time. As the meat cooks the milk will curdle, forming soft brown nuggets. Spoon these on top of the pork.

Serve in thick slices with braised fennel.

❧ *Pear and Almond Tart* ❧

Serves 10–12

PASTRY
225 g (8 oz) plain flour
a pinch of salt
175 g (6 oz) unsalted butter,
　　chilled and diced
100 g (4 oz) caster sugar
2 egg yolks

FILLING
225 g (8 oz) flaked almonds
225 g (8 oz) unsalted butter,
　　softened
225 g (8 oz) caster sugar
3 eggs
2 tablespoons Amaretto
5 ripe Comice pears

For the pastry, pulse the flour, salt, butter and sugar in a food processor until the mixture is coarsely combined. Add the egg yolks and pulse until the mixture combines evenly and leaves the sides of the bowl. Wrap in cling film and chill in the refrigerator for at least 1 hour until hard.

Pre-heat the oven to gas mark 4, 350°F (180°C).

Coarsely grate the pastry into a 30 cm (12 in) loose-bottomed French fluted flan tin, then press it evenly on to the sides and base of the tin. Cover the pastry with foil or greaseproof paper cut to fit and weigh it down with dried beans. Bake the pastry 'blind' for 20 minutes until lightly golden. Reduce the oven temperature to gas mark 3, 325°F (160°C). Leave the pastry to cool, then remove the beans very carefully.

Meanwhile, make the filling. Grind the flaked almonds in a food processor and set to one side. Cream the butter and sugar in the food processor until the mixture is pale, then add the ground almonds and continue to mix to a smooth paste. Add the eggs and Amaretto and pulse together until evenly incorporated.

Peel, halve and core the pears and arrange them cut-side down in the pastry case. Spread the almond mixture over the top and bake for 50–60 minutes until golden-brown and lightly set. Serve warm or cold.

❧ Pears Baked with Marsala ❧ and Cinnamon

Serves 4

4 Comice pears
40 g (1½ oz) butter, softened
25 g (1 oz) caster sugar
120 ml (4 fl oz) Marsala
50 ml (2 fl oz) white wine
2 cinnamon sticks

TO SERVE
Cream or crème fraiche

Pre-heat the oven to gas mark 6, 400°F (200°C).

Cut a small slice from the rounded end of each pear so that it will stand up, then remove the core. Stand the pears in an ovenproof dish. Spread a little butter on each pear and sprinkle with sugar. Pour the Marsala and white wine into the dish. Break up the cinnamon sticks and sprinkle these into the dish.

Bake for about 45 minutes until very tender and slightly shrivelled. Serve warm with cream or crème fraiche.

Anthony Tobin

AFTER FIVE YEARS with Nico Ladenis, latterly at Very Simply Nico, Anthony Tobin runs the kitchen at *South Lodge* in Sussex, a late Victorian country house hotel with a garden that sports the biggest rhododendron in England. His cooking still shows the influence of his mentor, while the style of the hotel encourages an interest in British food – particularly traditional puddings. These are simple in concept, made with the finest ingredients – and wickedly delicious. He is spreading his wings, however, to encompass new ideas and inspirations: his salmon pizza, a constant surprise to those who order it; his tiny chicken and leek pies, top sellers at lunchtime; and lamb fillet, rolled and baked in a roesti potato crust.

Anthony first came to cooking when he was fourteen, spending his nights after school working in a tiny pub-restaurant in the Midlands. He loves cooking, and his kitchen at South Lodge is unusually quiet and peaceful, a matter of some surprise to new members of his team. He firmly believes that a chef who is enthusiastic and relaxed, with a brigade similarly inclined, will produce better food. He is proving it.

Anthony Tobin with, clockwise from left: Baby Pie of Chicken, Leek and Morels (page 222), Caramelised Rice Pudding with Cinnamon Custard (page 231) and Salmon Pizza (page 218).

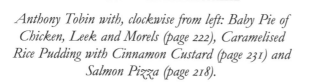

❧ Salmon Pizzas ❧
Fish Cream Sauce

Makes 4 pizzas

1 tablespoon olive oil plus extra
    for brushing
8 shallots, finely chopped
12 large basil leaves
1 × 425 g (15 oz) tin chopped
    tomatoes, drained
1 tablespoon tomato purée
50 ml (2 fl oz) white wine
salt and freshly ground black
    pepper

900 g (2 lb) fresh salmon fillet
100 g (4 oz) button mushrooms,
    thickly sliced
4 teaspoons tarragon leaves
4 teaspoons chopped chives
4 tomatoes, peeled, de-seeded
    and diced
225 g (8 oz) mozzarella cheese,
    coarsely grated

TO SERVE
Fish Cream Sauce (below)
coarsely ground sea salt

Line baking trays with baking parchment and brush with olive oil.

In a saucepan, heat the olive oil and cook the shallots in it with the basil until transparent. Add the chopped tomatoes, tomato purée and wine, then cook rapidly for about 15 minutes until the mixture is reduced to a thick sauce. Pass through a fine sieve and season to taste with salt and black pepper. Leave the sauce to cool.

Pre-heat the oven to gas mark 8, 450°F (230°C).

Cut the salmon fillet into 20 angled slices. They should taper from a thickness of about 5 mm (¼ in) thick. Reserve the trimmings. Arrange the salmon slices on the baking trays to form pizza bases about 15 cm (6 in) in diameter. The thicker edges must be on the outside. Use the salmon trimmings to fill in the centres of the bases. Spoon a little tomato sauce on each one and spread almost to the edge. Sprinkle with the mushrooms, tarragon, chives, diced tomato and mozzarella cheese. Bake in the oven for 8–10 minutes.

To serve, pour a little Fish Cream Sauce around each pizza, sprinkle with sea salt and serve immediately.

Fish Cream Sauce

40 g (1½ oz) unsalted butter
10 shallots, finely chopped
1 sprig of thyme
1 sprig of rosemary
120 ml (4 fl oz) white wine
50 ml (2 fl oz) dry vermouth
600 ml (1 pint) good fish stock

salt and freshly ground black
    pepper
2 leeks, white parts only, finely
    chopped
300 ml (10 fl oz) double cream
4 tablespoons finely chopped
    chives

Melt 15 g (½ oz) of the butter in a saucepan and cook the shallots and herbs over gentle heat until the shallots are transparent. Add the wine and vermouth and boil until completely evaporated. Add the fish stock, salt and black pepper and bring to the boil, then reduce to one-third by fast boiling.

Meanwhile, just cover the leeks with water and the remaining butter and cook rapidly until all the water has evaporated leaving the buttery juices. Press the leeks in a fine strainer to extract the juices and add the leeks to the sauce.

Stir in the cream and simmer very gently for about 30 minutes until the sauce is thick enough to coat the back of a wooden spoon. Remove from the heat and stir in half of the chives. Leave to infuse for 20 minutes. Pass through a fine sieve. Stir in the remaining chives and warm gently.

Cocottes of Smoked Haddock
Poached Eggs and Spinach, Hollandaise Sauce, Fish Cream Sauce

Serves 6

600 ml (1 pint) milk
1 bay leaf
2 sprigs of thyme
2 small cloves garlic
450 g (1 lb) naturally smoked
    haddock fillet

150 ml (5 fl oz) double cream
2 egg yolks
salt and freshly ground black
    pepper
a pinch of cayenne pepper
1 tablespoon chopped chives

TO SERVE
Spinach (see p. 220)
6 poached eggs
Hollandaise Sauce (see p. 220)
Fish Cream Sauce (opposite)

Place the milk, herbs and garlic in a wide, shallow pan. Add the haddock, then bring to the boil and poach for 2 minutes. Leave to cool. Remove the fish from the milk and flake the flesh, discarding the skin and bones. Add the cream and egg yolks and season with a little salt, if wishes – it depends on how salty the fish is – black pepper and the cayenne pepper. Stir in the chives.

Pre-heat the oven to gas mark 6, 400°F (200°C).

Butter 6 × 100 ml (3½ fl oz) ramekin dishes and divide the fish mixture between them. Cover with buttered foil and cook in the oven in a bain-marie for about 15 minutes. Alternatively, cover with cling film, pierce the top and cook in the microwave oven on high setting for about 4 minutes until lightly set. Leave to rest for a couple of minutes.

To serve, divide the spinach into 6 equal portions and set 1 portion in the centre of each warm plate. Shape it into a neat round, use a salad ring or 7.5 cm–10 cm (3 in–4 in) metal ring as a guide if necessary. Unmould the haddock cocottes and set 1 on top of each bed of spinach, then place a poached egg on top. Spoon a little Hollandaise Sauce on each egg and pour some Fish Cream Sauce around each portion. Serve at once.

Spinach

1.5 kg (3 lb) fresh spinach
40 g (1½ oz) clarified butter
salt and freshly ground black
    pepper

Wash the spinach and remove the stalks. Blanch in boiling, salted water, then drain thoroughly and squeeze out excess moisture. Warm the butter and add the spinach. Toss well and season to taste with salt and black pepper.

Hollandaise Sauce

4 shallots, finely chopped	3 egg yolks
1 sprig of tarragon	200 g (7 oz) unsalted butter,
3 white peppercorns, crushed	melted
50 ml (2 fl oz) white wine	cayenne pepper to taste
2 tablespoons white wine	salt and freshly ground black
vinegar	pepper

Place the shallots, tarragon, peppercorns, wine and vinegar in a saucepan and boil rapidly to reduce to about 1 tablespoon. Pass through a fine sieve into a bowl and add 2–3 tablespoons water and the egg yolks. Set the bowl over a saucepan of simmering water and whisk vigorously until the egg yolks thicken sufficiently to hold the trail of the whisk. Remove from the heat and whisk in the butter a little at a time. Season to taste with cayenne pepper, salt and black pepper. Keep warm.

Anthony Tobin's Cocotte of Smoked Haddock
with Poached Eggs and Spinach, Hollandaise Sauce
and Fish Cream Sauce (page 219).

❧ Baby Pies of ❧ Chicken, Leek and Morels

Makes 4 pies

500 g (1 lb 4 oz) shortcrust
    pastry
1–2 egg yolks, beaten
15 g (½ oz) unsalted butter
2 skinless, boneless chicken
    breasts, cut into 2.5 cm (1 in)
    dice
4 shallots, finely diced
2 medium-size leeks, cut into 2.5
    cm (1 in) dice
2 tablespoons roughly chopped
    tarragon leaves

2 tablespoons finely chopped
    chives
20 dried morels, covered with
    boiling water and soaked for
    30 minutes, then drained
50 ml (2 fl oz) Riesling wine
150 ml (5 fl oz) chicken stock
150 ml (5 fl oz) double cream
salt and freshly ground black
    pepper

TO SERVE
cooked vegetables, to garnish
chicken gravy

Pre-heat the oven to gas mark 7, 425°F (220°C).

You will need 4 metal rings about 7.5 cm (3 in) in diameter and 5 cm (2 in) high in which to bake the pies.

On a lightly floured surface, roll out the pastry to a thickness of 3 mm (⅛ in) and, using one of the metal rings as a guide, cut out 4 strips of pastry the exact circumference and height of the ring. Then use the ring to stamp out 8 rounds to make the bases and lids of the pies. Use a strip of pastry to line the inside of each ring, sealing the join with egg yolk. Brush the edge of a round and set this in the ring to make a base. Seal the edges well with egg yolk. Repeat with the remaining rings. Set the rings on a baking tray and chill in the refrigerator for at least 20 minutes.

Place a piece of greaseproof paper filled with dried beans inside each pastry case and bake the pastry blind for 10 minutes. Remove the beans. Allow the pastry cases to cool, then remove the rings and brush the outside of the cases with egg yolk. Return to the oven for 5 minutes to brown the outside. Leave to go cold, then replace the rings.

Melt the butter in a non-stick frying-pan and sauté the diced chicken until lightly coloured on all sides. Add the shallots and leeks and continue to fry gently. Stir in the herbs and morels, then add the white wine and stock and finally the cream. Bring to the boil, then simmer until the cream is reduced to a sauce consistency. Season to taste with salt and black pepper and leave to cool.

Fill the pastry cases with the chicken mixture. Brush the pastry lids with egg yolk, then press the lids on top of the filling, egg-side down, and seal well. Remove the pastry rings. Make a small hole in the centre of each lid. Brush the surface of the pies with egg yolk. Bake for about 20 minutes at the same temperature as before until golden-brown.

To serve, set each pie in the centre of a warm plate and garnish with a selection of vegetables. Spoon a little chicken gravy around each pie.

❧ *Spicy Chicken Sausage* ❧
Caramelised Apple Wedges, Cream and Calvados Sauce

Serves 4 as a starter, 2 as a main course

60 ml (4 tablespoons) milk
60 ml (4 tablespoons) double
   cream
1 small onion, finely chopped
1 bay leaf
1 teaspoon ground allspice
a generous pinch of ground
   white pepper

4 slices white bread, crusts
   removed
250 g (9 oz) skinless, boneless
   chicken breast, diced
1 egg white
salt and freshly ground black
   pepper
clarified butter for frying

TO SERVE
Caramelised Apple Wedges (see p. 224)
Cream and Calvados Sauce (see p. 224)

Place the milk, cream, onion, bay leaf, allspice and white pepper in a small saucepan and bring to the boil. Remove from the heat and leave to infuse for 20 minutes. Dice the bread, then strain the milk on to it and mix to a pulp. Leave to stand for 15 minutes. In a food processor, whiz the chicken breast and egg white for about 1 minute. Add the bread pulp, salt and black pepper and whiz until smooth. Chill in the refrigerator for 1 hour.

Divide the mixture into 4 portions. Wrap each one in a large piece of cling film and shape into a 'sausage'. Twist the ends tightly and tie securely. Place the sausages in a saucepan of boiling water and set a small lid on top of them to keep them under the water. Simmer for about 15 minutes until firm to the touch. Drain and chill in the refrigerator for 1 hour. Unwrap the sausages and fry in a frying-pan in the clarified butter until golden-brown. Keep warm. Use the frying-pan and butter for the Caramelised Apple Wedges.

To serve, cut each sausage into 4 or 5 pieces and set on a warm plate with 3 Caramelised Apple Wedges. Spoon some Cream and Calvados Sauce around each portion.

Caramelised Apple Wedges
clarified butter from the
        sausages (see main recipe)
2 teaspoons icing sugar
2 apples, peeled, cored and each
        cut into 6 wedges

Add the icing sugar and then the apple wedges to the frying-pan in which the sausages were fried. Fry until the apples are golden-brown and caramelised, but not too soft.

Cream and Calvados Sauce
200 ml (7 fl oz) double cream
2 teaspoons icing sugar
2 teaspoons Calvados

Warm all the ingredients in a small saucepan.

Calves Liver With Onions and Bacon Braised in Cassis

Serves 4

225 g (8 oz) silverskin button
        onions (preferably frozen)
400 ml (14 fl oz) red wine
150 ml (5 fl oz) crème de cassis
50 g (2 oz) clarified butter
175 g (6 oz) piece smoked bacon
        (or Italian speck), cut into
        lardons

3–4 large slices calves liver
        about 1 cm (½ in) thick, cut
        into 2.5 cm (1 in) strips
300 ml (10 fl oz) veal stock
salt and freshly ground black
        pepper
chopped parsley, to garnish

Place the onions, 300 ml (10 fl oz) of the red wine and 120 ml (4 fl oz) of the crème de cassis in a saucepan. Simmer for about 30 minutes until the onions are tender and dark red in colour and there is no liquid left in the pan. Leave to cool.

Heat the butter in a large frying-pan and cook the bacon until golden. Remove from the pan. Add the liver to the frying-pan and brown quickly on all sides. Remove from the frying-pan. Add the remaining wine and crème de cassis to the frying-pan and bubble to soften any sediment, stirring constantly. Add the veal stock and bring to the boil. Season with salt and black pepper, then boil until reduced to a coating consistency. Return the liver and bacon to the frying-pan, then stir in the onions and simmer until just warmed. Adjust seasoning to taste.

Serve at once in warm soup plates, garnished with chopped parsley.

Fillet of Lamb Baked in a Potato Crust
Tomato and Basil Sauce

Serves 2

450 g (1 lb) potatoes, coarsely
    grated
a pinch of salt
a pinch of cayenne pepper
2 tablespoons chopped basil

50 g (2 oz) clarified butter
fillet from a best end of lamb,
    trimmed of all fat and sinew
olive oil

TO SERVE
Tomato and Basil Sauce
    (see p. 226)

Mix the potatoes with the salt, cayenne pepper and basil. Leave for a few minutes, then squeeze out the excess liquid with your hands or with a clean tea-towel. Heat half of the butter in a small, preferably non-stick, frying-pan and spread half of the potato in a layer on the base of the frying-pan. Press the potato down well. Cook for a few minutes on one side only over moderate heat until golden, then turn out – cooked-side up – on to a large piece of buttered foil. Repeat with the remaining butter and potato mixture to make a second pancake. Flatten the pancakes with the base of the frying-pan.

Cut the lamb in two crossways and set a piece on each potato pancake. Roll the meat up inside the pancake and wrap tightly in the foil, like a Christmas cracker. Chill in the refrigerator for about 1 hour, then remove the foil.

Pre-heat the oven to gas mark 8, 450°F (230°C).

Heat about 1 cm (½ in) of olive oil in a frying-pan and fry the lamb parcels in it over medium heat until they are a rich golden colour all over. Set them on a wire tray over a baking tray and cook in the oven for 10–15 minutes, depending on how pink you like your meat. Leave to rest for about 15 minutes in a warm place.

Cut the lamb parcels in half and set 2 pieces on each warm plate. Spoon some Tomato and Basil Sauce over each portion and serve at once.

Tomato and Basil Sauce
300 ml (10 fl oz) veal stock (or
    lamb stock)
50 ml (2 fl oz) dry white wine
2 tablespoons peeled, de-seeded
    and diced tomato
2 tablespoons chopped basil
salt and freshly ground black
    pepper

Place the veal stock in a saucepan with the wine and boil rapidly until reduced to a sauce consistency. Stir in the tomatoes and basil and season to taste with salt and black pepper.

❧ Roast Saddle of Lamb ❧ with Provençale Herbs
Potato Galettes, Tomato and Rosemary Sauce

Serves 4

1 short cut saddle of lamb
    (approx. 1.25 – 1.5 kg/ 2½ –
    3 lb), boned – reserve all
    bones and trimmings for
    the sauce
1 tablespoon dried Herbes de
    Provence
about 3 tablespoons olive oil
salt and freshly ground black
    pepper

TO SERVE
Potato Galettes (opposite)
Tomato and Rosemary Sauce
    (opposite)

Pre-heat the oven to gas mark 8, 450°F (230°C).

Trim off the excess fat from the saddle leaving a thin layer of fat all around the joint. Sprinkle the herbs over the surface of the meat and drizzle with 1 tablespoon of the olive oil, and salt and black pepper. Roll and tie the joint tightly with string. In a large frying-pan, brown the lamb on all sides in the remaining oil until the fat is an even colour all round. Transfer the joint to a roasting tin and roast the meat for 25–30 minutes, turning now and again to ensure even cooking. Wrap in foil and leave to rest for 20 minutes before cutting into 4 thick slices.

To serve, place a Potato Galette on each warm plate and top with a slice of lamb. Pour some Tomato and Rosemary Sauce over each portion and serve at once.

Potato Galettes

450 g (1 lb) potatoes, coarsely
    grated
salt and freshly ground black
    pepper
50 g (2 oz) clarified butter

Mix the potatoes with salt and black pepper. Leave for a few minutes, then squeeze out the excess liquid with your hands or with a clean tea-towel. Heat the butter in a large frying-pan and, if wished, set 4 × 9 cm (3½ in) metal rings in the frying-pan. Spoon the potato into the rings and press down firmly. Cook for 12–15 minutes over moderate heat, turning once, until the potatoes are golden-brown on both sides. Remove from the rings.

Tomato and Rosemary Sauce

1–2 tablespoons olive oil
lamb bones and trimmings (see
    main recipe)
1 carrot, diced
1 small onion, diced
1 celery stalk, diced
1 leek, diced

2 cloves garlic
1 large sprig of rosemary
1 × 225 g (8 oz) tin tomatoes
1 tablespoon tomato purée
50 ml (2 fl oz) dry white wine
600 ml (1 pint) veal stock (or
    gravy)

Heat the olive oil in a large saucepan and brown the lamb bones and trimmings in it. Add the carrot, onion, celery, leek, garlic and rosemary and cook until well browned. Stir in the tomatoes, tomato purée, wine, stock and 300 ml (10 fl oz) water and bring to the boil. Simmer for 1 hour until the stock has reduced to a rich sauce. Strain through a fine sieve.

❧ *Light Chocolate* ❧ *Sponge Puddings*
Hot Chocolate Sauce

Serves 8

100 g (4 oz) dark chocolate,
    melted
finely grated rind of 1 orange
6 eggs, separated
100 g (4 oz) caster sugar
100 g (4 oz) ground almonds
50 g (2 oz) chocolate cake
    crumbs

TO SERVE
Hot Chocolate Sauce (below)

Pre-heat the oven to gas mark 4, 350°F (180°C). Butter and sugar the insides of 8 × 175 ml (6 fl oz) (approx.) metal pudding moulds.

In a bowl, mix the melted chocolate and grated orange rind together. In another bowl, whisk the egg yolks and caster sugar together until thick and pale, then fold the chocolate thoroughly into the mixture. Fold in the ground almonds and then the cake crumbs. Whisk the egg whites until stiff, then fold into the chocolate mixture. Divide the mixture between the prepared pudding moulds and cover with rounds of buttered foil. Bake in the oven in a bain-marie for about 20 minutes, until risen and just firm to the touch.

To serve, unmould the puddings on to warm plates and spoon a little Hot Chocolate Sauce over each one.

Hot Chocolate Sauce
300 ml (10 fl oz) double cream
150 g (5 oz) dark chocolate,
    broken into small pieces.

In a small saucepan, bring the cream just to the boil, then add the chocolate. Whisk until melted.

❧ Baked Apple Charlottes ❧
Caramel Sauce

Serves 4

12 thin slices white bread, crusts
  removed
100 g (4 oz) unsalted butter
1 egg, beaten
2 tablespoons demerara sugar
a pinch of ground cinnamon
a pinch of ground mixed spice

1 tablespoon chopped stem
  ginger
1 tablespoon stem ginger syrup
4 green dessert apples, peeled,
  cored and each cut into 8
  wedges

TO SERVE
Caramel Sauce (below)

Pre-heat the oven to gas mark 6, 400°F (200°C).

Using a rolling pin, roll the bread slices as thinly as possible. From 1 slice, cut 4 rounds to fit in the bases of 4 × 175 ml (6 fl oz) (approx.) metal pudding moulds. Trim the remaining slices to neaten the edges and cut each one into 3 strips. Melt 25 g (1 oz) of the butter and brush the moulds generously with it, then place a round of bread on the base of each mould. Brush with beaten egg. Brush each strip of bread with beaten egg and line each mould with 8 strips, egg-side inside. Arrange the slices so that they slightly overlap each other and cover the sides. They must come well above the rim of the mould.

Melt the remaining butter in a frying-pan and add the sugar, cinnamon, mixed spice, chopped ginger and ginger syrup, then cook gently for 1 minute, stirring all the time. Add the apple wedges and cook for 2−3 minutes until just tender and pliable. Remove from the heat.

Place the bread-lined pudding moulds in the oven for 2−3 minutes to just set the egg, then press in the apple wedges and add all the buttery juices. Fold the flaps of bread over to form a lid and trim as necessary. Bake for 20 minutes until the bread is crisp and golden.

To serve, unmould the apple charlotte on to warmed places and spoon some Caramel Sauce over.

Caramel Sauce
250 g (9 oz) sugar
½ vanilla pod, split
300 ml (10 fl oz) double cream

Place the sugar in a heavy-based saucepan and allow to caramelise to a rich golden colour. Shake the saucepan occasionally but do not stir the sugar. Brush down the sides with water to prevent any crystallisation.

Scrape the seeds from the vanilla pod and discard the pod. Place the cream and vanilla seeds in a saucepan and bring to the boil. Once the sugar has caramelised, remove the caramel from the heat and slowly pour into the hot cream. Whisk until smooth, then pass through a fine metal sieve.

🌼 *Toffee Sponge Puddings* 🌼
Caramel Sauce, Custard Sauce

Serves 8

175 g (6 oz) butter
175 g (6 oz) caster sugar
3 eggs
225 g (8 oz) plain flour
1 tablespoon baking powder
50 ml (2 fl oz) milk

TO SERVE
Caramel Sauce (see p. 229)
Custard Sauce (follow the recipe
    for Cinnamon Custard,
    opposite, but replace the
    bay leaf and cinnamon with
    a split vanilla pod.)

Pre-heat the oven to gas mark 4, 350°F (180°C) or prepare a steamer. Butter the insides of 8 × 175 ml (6 fl oz) metal pudding moulds.

In a bowl, cream the butter and sugar until light and fluffy, then beat in the eggs one at a time. Add a little of the measured flour if necessary to prevent the mixture curdling. Sift the flour and baking powder together and fold into the creamed mixture. Add the milk to give a soft dropping consistency. Divide the mixture between the prepared pudding moulds and cover with rounds of buttered foil. Bake in the oven in a bain-marie for 35–40 minutes until risen and firm to the touch. Alternatively, cook in a steamer for the same length of time.

To serve, unmould the puddings on to warm plates. Serve with a little Caramel Sauce poured over each one and Custard Sauce poured around.

❧ *Caramelised Rice Puddings* ❧
Cinnamon Custard

Serves 6

2 vanilla pods, split
300 ml (10 fl oz) double cream
300 ml (10 fl oz) milk
rind of ½ lemon

150 g (5 oz) pudding rice
300 g (11 oz) sugar
2 eggs, separated

TO SERVE
Cinnamon Custard (below)

Pre-heat the oven to gas mark 2, 300°F (150°C).

Scrape the seeds from the vanilla pods. In an ovenproof saucepan, bring the cream and milk to the boil with the lemon rind and the vanilla seeds and pods. Stir in the rice and cover with greaseproof paper. Bake in the oven for about 30 minutes until tender. Remove the rice from the oven, stir in 100 g (4 oz) of the sugar and leave to cool.

In a saucepan, dissolve the remaining sugar over medium heat, then boil to a rich caramel colour. Pour the caramel into 6 × 250 ml (8 fl oz) metal pudding moulds, carefully swirling it around the sides. Leave to go cold.

Remove the lemon rind and vanilla pod from the rice and beat in the egg yolks. Whisk the egg whites until stiff, then fold into the rice. Divide between the caramel-lined moulds and cover with pieces of buttered foil. Bake for about 25 minutes, at the same temperature as before, until risen and just firm to the touch.

To serve, unmould on to warm plates and spoon a generous amount of Cinnamon Custard around each portion.

Cinnamon Custard
600 ml (1 pint) milk
1 bay leaf
1 cinnamon stick
5 egg yolks
65 g (2½ oz) sugar

Place the milk, bay leaf and cinnamon in a saucepan and bring to the boil. Whisk the egg yolks and sugar until pale, then stir the milk into the mixture. Stir well and return to the saucepan. Cook over very gentle heat, stirring all the time, until the mixture is thick enough to coat the back of a wooden spoon. Pass through a fine sieve.

Antony Worrall Thompson

NOW CHEF-PATRON of the London club, *One Ninety Queens-gate*, the adjoining and cheerful *Bistrot 190*, and his new restaurant *Dell'ugo*, Antony Worrall Thompson remembers cooking scrambled eggs for his mother's breakfast at the age of five. A later culinary exploit had him catching a duck on the river and roasting it, feathers and all. After refining his techniques a little, he chose to turn from catering management back to the kitchen, his true vocation. Several years later he opened Ménage à Trois, a pretty restaurant serving unashamedly pretty food, and the only one in London to offer nothing but starters and puddings. Its menu features the three little filo pastry parcels on which the restaurant's name was based.

Antony has always cooked what he likes to eat, and the style in both One Ninety and the less expensive Bistrot leans towards the Italian. Dishes range from simple classics like calves liver with polenta, to hearty and gutsy country dishes such as lamb shank with pesto, cabbage and olive oil potato purée — food from the heart.

Completely self-taught, he loves eating, researching and talking about food, and is one of only three chefs to have been awarded cuisine's Oscar, '*Meilleur Ouvrier de Grande-Bretagne*', a title awarded by the French.

(Overleaf) Antony Worrall Thompson with, clockwise from left: Braised Lamb Shanks with Garlic, Rosemary and Flageolet Beans (page 244), Chilled Tomato Bisque with Char-grilled Vegetables (page 234), Bloody Mary (page 249) and Marinated Field Mushrooms with Grilled Baby Leeks (page 245).

❧ *Filo Pastry Parcels* ❧

Makes about 48 parcels

12 sheets filo pastry approx.
50 cm × 25 cm
(20 in × 10 in)
100–150 g (4–5 oz) unsalted
butter, melted
oil for deep-frying
choice of fillings

Set 1 sheet of pastry in front of you with a long side towards you and keep the remaining sheets covered with a damp, clean cloth. Cut the sheet into 4 vertical strips approximately 12.5 cm × 25 cm (5 in × 10 in). Brush with melted butter and fold each strip in half to make 4 squares about 12.5 cm (5 in) across. Brush each square with melted butter.

Place a dessertspoon of filling in the centre of each pastry square, then bring the corners up over the filling and pinch them together to form parcels. Place on an oiled tray and chill in the refrigerator for at least 30 minutes before cooking. Repeat the process with the remaining 11 sheets of pastry.

Heat the oil in a large saucepan or deep-fryer. Deep-fry the parcels for about 2 minutes until crisp and golden. You will need to do this in batches of about 6 at a time. Drain on absorbent paper and serve at once. Alternatively, bake the parcels in an oven pre-heated to gas mark 6, 400°F (200°C) for 10–15 minutes until golden. The parcels can be re-heated in the oven after deep-frying, if wished

Cheese and Spinach Filling
Sufficient for 24 parcels

450 g (1 lb) fresh spinach, stalks removed
50 g (2 oz) unsalted butter
1 shallot, finely chopped
1 clove garlic, crushed
4 tablespoons béchamel sauce
½ garlic Boursin cheese
salt and freshly ground black pepper

Blanch the spinach in boiling salted water, then drain and squeeze out the moisture in a clean tea-towel. Melt the butter in a small frying-pan and gently cook the shallot and garlic until softened but not coloured. Place in a food processor with the béchamel sauce, cheese, salt and black pepper and blend until smooth. Leave to go cold.

Cheese and Leek Filling

Sufficient for 24 parcels

25 g (1 oz) unsalted butter
1 shallot, finely chopped
1 clove garlic, crushed
225 g (8 oz) leeks, finely chopped
2 teaspoons thyme leaves

4 tablespoons béchamel sauce
100 g (4 oz) Roquefort cheese, crumbled
salt and freshly ground black pepper

Melt the butter in a small saucepan and gently cook the shallot, garlic and leeks until softened but not coloured. Add the thyme, then remove from the heat. Stir in the béchamel sauce and then the cheese and salt and pepper and blend in a food processor until smooth. Leave to go cold.

Cheese and Cranberry Filling

Sufficient for 24 parcels

700 g (1½ lb) Camembert cheese, rind removed

8 tablespoons cranberry sauce
cayenne pepper

Place a small piece of Camembert cheese in the centre of each pastry square. Top with 1 teaspoon cranberry sauce and a pinch of cayenne pepper.

❧ *Chilled Tomato Bisque* ❧
Char-grilled Vegetables, Virgin Olive Oil

Serves 4

1 red pepper, quartered and de-seeded
2 slices (approx. 40 g/ 1½ oz) white country bread, crusts removed
1 tablespoon sherry vinegar
1 clove garlic, finely chopped
2 teaspoons caster sugar
1 red chilli, de-seeded and finely diced
50 ml (2 fl oz) extra virgin olive oil plus extra for serving

450 g (1 lb) plum tomatoes, liquidised and strained
1 tablespoon tomato ketchup
1 × 425 g (15 oz) tin tomato juice
4 spring onions, finely sliced
½ cucumber, peeled and diced
1 tablespoon pesto
salt and freshly ground black pepper

TO SERVE
4 portions Char-grilled Vegetables (see p. 236)
virgin olive oil
freshly ground black pepper

Pre-heat the grill to high. Lay the red pepper on a baking tray and grill until charred. Peel the pepper. Crumble the bread into a food processor and add the vinegar, garlic, sugar and chilli. With the liquidiser running, add the olive oil. Then add the liquidised tomatoes, tomato ketchup, tomato juice, spring onions, cucumber, red pepper and pesto. Blend until a rough soup consistency. Season to taste with salt and black pepper.

To serve, arrange a portion of Char-grilled Vegetables in the centre of each bowl. Pour some bisque around and dribble olive oil over the surface. Season with black pepper.

Char-grilled Vegetables

1 small aubergine, cut lengthways into 4 slices and sprinkled with salt

1 courgette, cut lengthways into 4 slices

4 spring onions, blanched for 2 minutes

1 yellow pepper, quartered and de-seeded

4 asparagus stalks, trimmed

4–6 tablespoons olive oil

MARINADE

120 ml (4 fl oz) olive oil

½ small red onion, finely diced

1 clove garlic, finely chopped

½–1 red chilli, de-seeded and finely chopped

1 tablespoon pesto

1 tablespoon sherry vinegar

salt and freshly ground black pepper

For the marinade, mix the olive oil, onion, garlic, chilli, pesto and sherry vinegar in a wide, shallow dish and season to taste with salt and black pepper.

Pre-heat the grill to high. Rinse and dry the aubergine slices.

Dip all vegetables in the olive oil then grill on both sides for 2–3 minutes, or until lightly charred but not very soft. Transfer to the marinade and leave for up to 24 hours in a cool place.

🌺 *Mussels in Saffron Broth* 🌺
Crostini with Clams

Serves 4

900 ml (1½ pints) fish stock
a pinch of saffron threads
4 tablespoons olive oil plus extra
    for serving
4 teaspoons sesame oil
2 teaspoons chilli oil
2 shallots, finely chopped
2 cloves garlic, crushed
2 tablespoons chopped
    coriander root
5 cm (2 in) piece fresh ginger,
    grated
2 red chillis, de-seeded and finely
    chopped

300 ml (10 fl oz) white wine
2 bay leaves
2 strips of orange peel
1 kg (2 lb) baby clams, cleaned
1 kg (2 lb) fresh mussels, cleaned
8 baby leeks
50 g (2 oz) mange tout
4 spring onions, sliced
1 small courgette, thinly sliced
12 cherry tomatoes, peeled
25 g (1 oz) bean sprouts
freshly ground black pepper

TO SERVE
Crostini with Clams (see p. 238)
deep-fried ginger julienne strips,
    to garnish

Place the fish stock in a large saucepan with the saffron and heat gently. Meanwhile, heat the olive, sesame and chilli oils in a very large saucepan (or use 2 saucepans and divide the flavouring ingredients between them). Add the shallots, garlic, coriander root, ginger and half of the chilli and cook until softened but not coloured. Add the white wine, bay leaves and orange peel and bring to the boil. Add the clams, cover and cook for 5 minutes. Add the mussels, cover and cook for a further 3–5 minutes until the shells start opening. Discard any mussels or clams which stay closed. (If you are using 2 saucepans, cook the clams in one for 8–10 minutes and the mussels in the other for 3–5 minutes.)

Remove the clams and mussels from the cooking liquid and leave to cool. Pass the cooking liquid through a very fine strainer or muslin into the fish stock. Remove the clams and mussels from their shells. Finely chop the clams. The clams will be used for the crostini.

Bring the fish stock to a simmer and add the leeks, mange tout, spring onions, courgettes, tomatoes, bean sprouts and the remaining chilli. Cook for 3–4 minutes until the vegetables are just tender. Add the mussels.

Serve the broth drizzled with olive oil and a sprinkling of black pepper with the Crostini with Clams, garnished with deep-fried ginger julienne strips on the side.

Crostini with Clams

1 whole garlic bulb
4 slices Italian country bread
olive oil
chopped clams (see main recipe)
1 tablespoon finely chopped
   orange rind

1 tablespoon finely chopped
   lemon rind
1 tablespoon grated fresh ginger
1 tablespoon chopped coriander
   leaves
1 teaspoon finely chopped red
   chilli

Pre-heat the oven to gas mark 6, 400°F (200°C).

Roast the garlic for 30 minutes. Drizzle the slices of bread with a little olive oil and bake for about 10 minutes until crisp.

Squeeze the garlic bulb to extract all the purée from the cloves and spread the purée on the crostini. Mix the chopped clams with the orange and lemon rind, ginger, coriander and chilli and pile on to the crostini.

❁ Spicy Crab Blinis ❁
Hollandaise Sauce, Poached Eggs

Makes about 20

120 g (4½ oz) cornmeal or
   polenta
65 g (2½ oz) plain flour
1½ teaspoons baking powder
1 teaspoon salt
½ teaspoon freshly ground black
   pepper
1 teaspoon ground cumin
1 teaspoon ground coriander
1 tablespoon extra virgin olive
   oil
½ teaspoon chilli oil
1 teaspoon sesame oil
2 eggs, separated

2 tablespoons freshly squeezed
   lime juice
3 tablespoons coriander leaves,
   chopped
3 tablespoons mint, chopped
3 tablespoons basil, chopped
2 small, red chillies, de-seeded
   and finely chopped
1 teaspoon finely chopped
   pickled ginger
300 ml (10 fl oz) milk
225 g (8 oz) white crabmeat
2 tablespoons finely chopped
   spring onions
clarified butter for frying

TO SERVE
Hollandaise Sauce (opposite)
poached eggs
white crabmeat and chopped
   herbs such as mint, basil and
   coriander, to garnish

In a food processor, combine the cornmeal, flour, baking powder, salt, black pepper, cumin and coriander and pulse quickly. With the machine still running, add the olive, chilli and sesame oils and the egg yolks and lime juice. Add the herbs, chilli and ginger and finally mix in the milk to make a fairly thick batter. Transfer the mixture to a bowl and stir in the crabmeat and spring onions. Cover and leave for 1 hour in a cool place.

Just before cooking the blini, whisk the egg whites until stiff and fold into the crabmeat mixture. Heat some clarified butter in a large frying-pan over medium-high heat and spoon about 4 tablespoons of the crabmeat mixture into the pan to make 4 blinis. Use a metal ring as a guide if you wish. Cook until the mixture is starting to set and then carefully turn each blini. Cook until the blinis are golden-brown on each side.

Serve each portion topped with a poached egg and Hollandaise Sauce, and garnished with a sprinkling of crabmeat and chopped herbs.

Hollandaise Sauce

Makes about 400 ml (14 fl oz)
5 tablespoons white wine
    vinegar
½ teaspoon white peppercorns,
    crushed
1 bay leaf
4 egg yolks
200 g (7 oz) unsalted butter,
    melted
salt

Boil the vinegar with 4 tablespoons water and the crushed peppercorns and bay leaf until reduced to 2 tablespoons. Strain into a double boiler. Stir in the egg yolks and whisk over very low heat until they gradually start to thicken. Remove from the heat and whisk in the butter in a thin stream. Add salt to taste. Cover the sauce with greaseproof paper and keep warm.

❧ *Salmon Rillettes* ❧ *with Roasted Peppers*

Serves 12

ROASTED PEPPERS

2 red peppers, de-seeded and
    quartered lengthways
1 shallot, diced
1 clove garlic, finely chopped
6 basil leaves, cut into julienne
    strips

4 tablespoons olive oil
1 tablespoon sherry vinegar
salt and freshly ground black
    pepper

SALMON RILLETTES

1 kg (2 lb) salmon fillet, skinned
about 2.25 litres (4 pints) court
    bouillon
4 shallots, finely chopped
450 g (1 lb) unsalted butter
1 teaspoon thyme leaves
2 tablespoons lemon juice
4 egg yolks
1 teaspoon freshly ground black
    pepper

generous pinch of grated
    nutmeg
a pinch of cayenne pepper
4 tablespoons double cream
450 g (1 lb) smoked salmon,
    diced
4 tablespoons chopped chives
100–175 g (4–6 oz) clarified
    butter

TO SERVE

toasted country bread
Keta caviar and Tapenade (see
    p. 242), to garnish

For the roasted peppers, pre-heat the grill to high, then place the peppers skin-side up under the grill and cook until lightly charred. Put them in a paper bag or foil pouch, and leave to cool for 10 minutes. Peel and dice the peppers, then place them in a bowl with the remaining ingredients and mix.

For the salmon rilettes, place the salmon in a wide, shallow saucepan and just cover it with the court bouillon. Bring just to the boil, then remove from the heat and leave to go cold. Flake the fish, removing any bones.

Cook the shallots in a small amount of the butter with the thyme, until softened but not coloured.

Place the flaked salmon in a food processor with the shallot mixture, remaining butter, lemon juice, egg yolks, black pepper, nutmeg, cayenne pepper and cream. Blend together using the pulse button until all the ingredients are incorporated but not smooth. Transfer to a bowl and fold in the smoked salmon, chives and roasted pepper mixture with all its juices. Pack into a terrine dish or loaf tin, smooth the surface and flood with clarified butter. Chill in the refrigerator until set.

Unmould the rillettes and cut into slices. Garnish each portion with a spoonful of Keta caviar and a spoonful of Tapenade. Serve with toasted country bread.

Tapenade
Makes 175–225 g (6–8 oz)

150 g (5 oz) stoned black olives	1 tablespoon Dijon mustard
6 tinned anchovy fillets (or	2 tablespoons capers
25 g/1 oz tinned tuna)	3 sun-dried tomatoes
2 cloves garlic, crushed	2–3 tablespoons olive oil
8 large basil leaves	freshly ground black pepper

Blend all the ingredients except the black pepper in a food processor until fairly smooth. Season to taste with the pepper.

🦴 *Pot Roast Pork Knuckle* 🦴
in Stout

Serves 4

2 × 1.5 kg (3 lb) pork knuckles from the shoulder	75 g (3 oz) unsalted butter
12 stoned black olives and 12 sage leaves	1 onion, finely sliced
or	1–2 tablespoons oil
6 stoned prunes, halved, and 12 tinned anchovy fillets	300 ml (10 fl oz) stout
	300 ml (10 fl oz) chicken stock

MARINADE

2 teaspoons black peppercorns, crushed	7 small cloves garlic
2 teaspoons salt	2 tablespoons soft brown sugar
2 teaspoons dried oregano	2 tablespoons olive oil
1 teaspoon thyme leaves	2 tablespoons wine vinegar

TO SERVE

roast carrots	
roast parsnips	Crostini (opposite) spread with
polenta mash	Tapenade (above), and deep-fried sage leaves, to garnish

For the marinade, combine the peppercorns, salt, herbs, garlic and sugar in a food processor then gradually add the oil and vinegar.

Remove the rind from each pork knuckle and keep to one side. Trim off the excess fat from the meat. Make 6 incisions in each piece of pork and press a black olive and sage leaf, or half a prune and an anchovy fillet, into each slit. Rub with the marinade and leave to marinate in a cool place for at least 3 hours.

Pre-heat the oven to gas mark 2, 300°F (150°C).

Melt the butter in a flameproof casserole and cook the onion over gentle heat until it caramelises. This will take about 20 minutes. In a separate pan, heat the oil and brown the meat well in it on all sides. Set the pork on top of the onion slices in the casserole. Add the stout to the pan in which the pork was browned and bring to the boil to soften any sediment in the pan. Add the stout, and all the residue from the pan, to the casserole with the chicken stock. Cover each piece of meat with its reserved rind then cover the casserole. Cook in the oven for about 3 hours until the meat is very tender and falling off the bone. Remove the meat from the bones and cut in chunks. Keep warm. Pour all the pan juices into a food processor and blend until smooth. Pour over the meat.

Garnish with Crostini spread with Tapenade and topped with deep-fried sage leaves. Serve with roast carrots, roast parsnips and polenta mash.

Crostini
4 slices Italian country bread
olive oil

Pre-heat the oven to gas mark 6, 400°F (200°C).

Drizzle the slices of bread with a little olive oil and bake for about 10 minutes until crisp.

Antony Worrall Thompson's Chocolate Terrine
with Fresh Figs in Raspberry and
Red Wine Sauce (page 246).

🍀 Braised Lamb Shanks 🍀 with Garlic, Rosemary and Flageolet Beans

Serves 4

2 × 1 kg (2 lb) lamb shanks
12 small sprigs of rosemary
12 slivers garlic

BRAISING INGREDIENTS
50 g (2 oz) goose fat (or butter
   or beef dripping)
2 carrots, roughly chopped
2 celery stalks, roughly chopped
1 leek, roughly chopped
1 onion, roughly chopped
1 head garlic, halved horizontally

SAUCE
100 g (4 oz) streaky bacon, cut
   into lardons and blanched
2 tablespoons extra virgin
   olive oil
½ carrot, finely diced
½ celery stalk, finely diced
½ onion, finely diced
6 cloves garlic
4 plum tomatoes, peeled and
   diced

GARNISH
2 tablespoons olive oil
100–175 (4–6 oz) bacon
   lardons

6 tinned anchovy fillets, halved
salt and freshly ground black
   pepper

½ bottle red wine
300 ml (10 fl oz) chicken stock
   (or lamb stock)
1 sprig of thyme
2 sprigs of rosemary
2 bay leaves
2 strips of dried orange peel

2 sprigs of thyme
Leaves from 2 sprigs of
   rosemary, chopped
1 × 410 g (14 oz) tin flageolet
   beans, drained (or
   100 g/4 oz dried flageolet
   beans, soaked overnight
   and then boiled rapidly for
   10 minutes)

100–175 (4–6 oz) button
   onions, boiled
12 cloves garlic
25 g (1 oz) unsalted butter

Pre-heat the oven to gas mark 2, 300°F (150°C).

Remove most of the fat from each shank, then scrape the meat away from the bone to loosen it. Make 6 deep incisions in each joint and insert a sprig of rosemary and a sliver of garlic wrapped in half an anchovy fillet into each incision. Season the meat with salt and black pepper. Heat the goose fat in a heatproof casserole and fry the meat in it until well browned on all sides. Remove the meat from the pan. Add the carrots, celery, leeks, onion and garlic and cook over a high heat until well browned. Add the red wine to the pan and bring to the boil, scraping any sediment from the bottom of the pan. Add the chicken stock, herbs and orange peel to the pan, then place the meat on top. Cover and cook in the oven for 2½ hours.

Meanwhile, start to prepare the sauce. Heat the olive oil in a saucepan and brown the bacon in it. Then reduce the heat and add the carrot, celery, onion and garlic and cook for 8 minutes until the vegetables are softened. Add the tomatoes, herbs and beans. Set aside.

When the lamb has finished cooking, remove the joints to a casserole and keep warm in a low oven (gas mark 1/250°F/140°C) with the oven door ajar. Blend the braising vegetables and their juices in a food processor, then pass the liquid through a sieve and add it to the bean mixture. Simmer, covered, for 1 hour. Remove the thyme stalks and season to taste with salt and black pepper. Just before the sauce finishes cooking, turn the oven up to gas mark 7, 425°F (220°C). Pour the sauce over the lamb joints and heat through in the oven for about 10 minutes.

For the garnish, heat the olive oil in a frying-pan with the butter, then fry the lardons, onions and garlic until lightly caramelised. Spoon over the meat just before serving.

Marinated Field Mushrooms with Grilled Baby Leeks
Crostini

Serves 4

450 g (1 lb) small field
    mushrooms, stalks removed
6 tablespoons extra virgin olive
    oil plus extra as required
1 teaspoon sesame oil
2 teaspoons soy sauce
2 tablespoons Chardonnay wine
½ red chilli, de-seeded and finely
    chopped
2 cloves garlic, sliced
1 teaspoon clear honey

2 tablespoons chopped mint
    leaves
2 tablespoons chopped
    coriander leaves
salt and freshly ground black
    pepper
12 bay leaves
pared rind of 2 oranges
16 baby leeks
seasoned olive oil for dipping

TO SERVE

8 Crostini (see p. 243), rubbed
    with a cut garlic clove

Tapenade (see p. 242) or pesto
grated rind of 2 oranges, to
    garnish

Wipe the mushrooms with a damp cloth.

Heat the olive and sesame oils in a large frying-pan and add the mushrooms in 1 layer, gill-side down. Cook for 2–3 minutes. Turn the mushrooms well in the oil, cover and cook slowly for 5–6 minutes.

Transfer the mushrooms to a shallow dish. Reserve the pan juices. Add the soy sauce, wine, chilli, garlic and honey to the pan and boil quickly until reduced a little. Remove from the heat and stir in the mint and coriander. Season to taste with salt and black pepper, adding extra olive oil if wished. Pour this dressing over the mushrooms.

Fill a steamer with water and place the bay leaves and orange rind in the top section. Steam for 5 minutes, then add the leeks and steam for a further 6 minutes. Remove the leeks from the steamer and dip them in enough seasoned olive oil to coat them. Grill for 3 minutes under high heat and return to the olive oil.

Garnish the mushrooms and leeks with the grated orange rind. Serve at room temperature with the Crostini spread with Tapenade or pesto.

❧ Chocolate Terrine ❧
Fresh Figs in Raspberry and Red Wine Sauce

Serves 10–12

10 dried figs
200 ml (7 fl oz) freshly made tea
50 ml (2 fl oz) brandy
500 ml (17 fl oz) double cream
175 g (6 oz) dark chocolate,
  broken into pieces

75 g (3 oz) unsalted butter
3 eggs, separated
40 g (1½ oz) caster sugar
20 g (¾ oz) cocoa powder

TO SERVE
Fresh Figs in Raspberry and
  Red Wine Sauce (opposite)

Soak the figs in the tea and brandy for at least 24 hours until they are plump. Drain thoroughly and chop roughly.

Line a 900 g (2 lb) loaf tin or terrine dish with oiled cling film. Whip 300 ml (8 fl oz) of the cream until stiff and carefully spread it on to the base and sides of the loaf tin or terrine dish. Freeze until firm.

Melt the chocolate with half of the butter in a bowl set over a saucepan of simmering water. Leave to cool slightly. Beat the egg yolks with the sugar until light and fluffy. Beat the remaining butter and cocoa powder together until light and fluffy. Fold the chocolate butter into the egg mixture, then fold this into the cocoa butter. Fold in the chopped figs.

Whisk the egg whites until they form soft peaks. Whisk the remaining cream until it forms soft peaks. Fold the cream and then the egg whites into the chocolate and fig mixture until evenly combined. Pour the mixture into the cream-lined loaf tin or terrine dish. Cover with foil or cling film and freeze for 4–6 hours, or preferably overnight, until solid.

Cut in thin slices and serve with Fresh Figs in Raspberry and Red Wine Sauce.

Fresh Figs in Raspberry and Red Wine Sauce

450 g (1 lb) raspberries
2 tablespoons lemon juice
150 g (5 oz) caster sugar
1 bottle red wine
300 ml (10 fl oz) orange juice

2 strips fresh orange peel, each
    studded with 1 clove
½ vanilla pod
1 bay leaf
10–12 fresh figs

Liquidise the raspberries with the lemon juice and sugar, then pass through a fine sieve.

Place the red wine, orange juice, orange peel studded with cloves, vanilla pod and bay leaf in a wide, shallow saucepan and bring to the boil. Add the raspberry purée. Add the fresh figs and poach for about 4 minutes until just tender. Remove the figs from the liquid and place in a shallow dish.

Bring the liquid to a fast boil and boil until it has reduced to a generous 300 ml (10 fl oz). Pour over the figs and leave to cool.

🌸 Mediterranean Sandwich 🌸

Serves 6–8

150 g (5 oz) aubergine, sliced
    lengthways
150 g (5 oz) courgette, sliced
    lengthways
120 ml (4 fl oz) olive oil
1 red pepper, quartered and
    de-seeded
1 yellow pepper, quartered and
    de-seeded
1 pugliese loaf (Italian round
    country bread)
1 clove garlic, halved
4 tablespoons Tapenade
    (see p. 242)

30 large basil leaves
150 g (5 oz) sun-dried tomatoes
4 tablespoons pesto
400 g (14 oz) buffalo mozzarella,
    thinly sliced
100 g (4 oz) stoned black olives
50 g (2 oz) red onion, thinly
    sliced
50 g (2 oz) rocket leaves
1 tablespoon balsamic vinegar
50 g (2 oz) spinach leaves
    (known as pousse)
salt and freshly ground black
    pepper

TO SERVE
warm potato salad

Lay the aubergine and courgette slices on a baking tray and drizzle with 2 tablespoons of the olive oil. Pre-heat the grill to high and cook the slices until they are lightly charred on both sides. Lay the peppers on a baking tray and grill until lightly charred all over. Peel the peppers.

Cut a lid off the top of the loaf and hollow out the bread, leaving a crust of about 2.5 cm (1 in) all the way round. Rub the cut surface of the bread and lid with the garlic, then drizzle with the remaining olive oil. Spread the tapenade on the bottom of the loaf then layer up all the ingredients in the order shown above, seasoning generously with salt and black pepper between each layer. Pour on the vinegar between the rocket leaves and spinach leaves. Replace the lid and wrap the loaf in cling film. Place in the refrigerator and leave pressed under a heavy weight overnight.

Serve the sandwich in wedges, with a warm potato salad.

🦋 *Individual Niçoise Sandwich* 🦋

Serves 1

1 ciabatta roll	½ tomato, halved
½ clove garlic	25 g (1 oz) tinned tuna
1 teaspoon olive oil	2 slices hard-boiled egg
salt and freshly ground black	1 slice red onion
pepper	2–3 basil leaves
1 teaspoon Tapenade	2 black olives, stoned
(see p. 242)	1 tablespoon anchovy dressing
6–8 French beans, cooked	(below)

Cut the roll in half and hollow out a little of the bread. Rub the cut surfaces with the garlic and drizzle with the olive oil. Season with salt and black pepper. Spread the base of the roll with the tapenade, then arrange all the remaining ingredients except the anchovy dressing on top of it. Drizzle with the anchovy dressing and replace the top half.

Wrap the roll in cling film and press down with a small weight. Chill until required.

ANCHOVY DRESSING
Makes about 300 ml (8 fl oz)

200 ml (7 fl oz) olive oil	4 tinned anchovy fillets
3 tablespoons balsamic vinegar	¾ teaspoon thyme leaves
1 tablespoon capers	freshly ground black pepper

Blend all the ingredients except the black pepper together in a food processor. Season to taste with the pepper. This dressing will keep for 2–3 weeks in the refrigerator.

❧ *Salmon and Bacon on Rye* ❧
My Favourite Sandwich

Serves 1

1 thick slice rye bread
25 g (1 oz) cream cheese
50 g (2 oz) smoked salmon,
   sliced
2 rashers streaky bacon, grilled
   until crisp

2 teaspoons mango chutney
1 thin slice red onion
2 teaspoons capers, deep-fried
   in hot oil until crisp

Spread the bread with the cream cheese. Arrange the smoked salmon on one half of the slice and the bacon on the other half. Top with the chutney, onion slice and deep-fried capers.

❧ *Bloody Mary* ❧

Serves 12

50 ml (2 fl oz) Worcestershire
   sauce
1 tablespoon tomato ketchup
1 teaspoon Tabasco sauce
1 teaspoon celery salt
65 ml (2½ fl oz) lemon juice
2 tablespoons orange juice
1 teaspoon freshly grated
   horseradish

1 teaspoon finely chopped
   shallot
½ teaspoon finely ground black
   pepper
1.75 litres (3 pints) V-8 vegetable
   juice (or tomato juice)
2 tablespoons dry sherry
300 ml (10 fl oz) vodka
   (preferably pepper vodka)
salt

TO SERVE
plenty of ice cubes
12 celery stalks with leaves

Place the first 11 ingredients in a liquidiser and blend thoroughly. Transfer to a jug, cover and leave in a cool place for 24 hours for the flavours to develop. Pass the mixture through a fine sieve, then stir in the vodka and season with salt to taste.

Divide the ice cubes among 12 glasses and top up with the mixture. Place a celery stalk in each glass and serve immediately.

Index

All recipes are listed by name in the Contents pages (5–13)